The Phantom [illegible] o a contained gallop, ma[illegible] his band. He pawed the [illegible]ing movements and his possessive snort carried to them.

Mine, he seemed to say. He waited for them to make the next move—if they dared.

Wordlessly, Jake and Kit began backing toward the truck, and Sam decided she should join them.

You win, boy, Sam thought, but she couldn't tear her eyes away.

Zanzibar, she thought longingly, but she wanted him to graze, to stay strong for the cold winter ahead, and she knew he wouldn't lower his head to eat while they stood watching him.

Read all the books about the

Phantom Stallion

1

THE WILD ONE

2

MUSTANG MOON

3

DARK SUNSHINE

4

THE RENEGADE

5

FREE AGAIN

6

THE CHALLENGER

7

DESERT DANCER

8

GOLDEN GHOST

9

GIFT HORSE

10

RED FEATHER FILLY

11

UNTAMED

12

RAIN DANCE

13

HEARTBREAK BRONCO

14

MOONRISE

15

KIDNAPPED COLT

16

THE WILDEST HEART

17

MOUNTAIN MARE

18

FIREFLY

19

SECRET STAR

20

BLUE WINGS

21

DAWN RUNNER

22

WILD HONEY

23

GYPSY GOLD

Phantom Stallion

24

Run Away Home

TERRI FARLEY

HarperTrophy®
An Imprint of HarperCollins*Publishers*

Run Away Home

 For information address HarperCollins Children's Books, a division of HarperCollins Publishers, 1350 Avenue of the Americas, New York, NY 10019.
www.harpercollinschildrens.com

Library of Congress Catalog Card Number: 2006920322
ISBN-10: 0-06-081541-8—ISBN-13: 978-0-06-081541-7

❖

First Harper Trophy edition, 2006

This book is dedicated to all the readers who ride the Phantom's range with me.

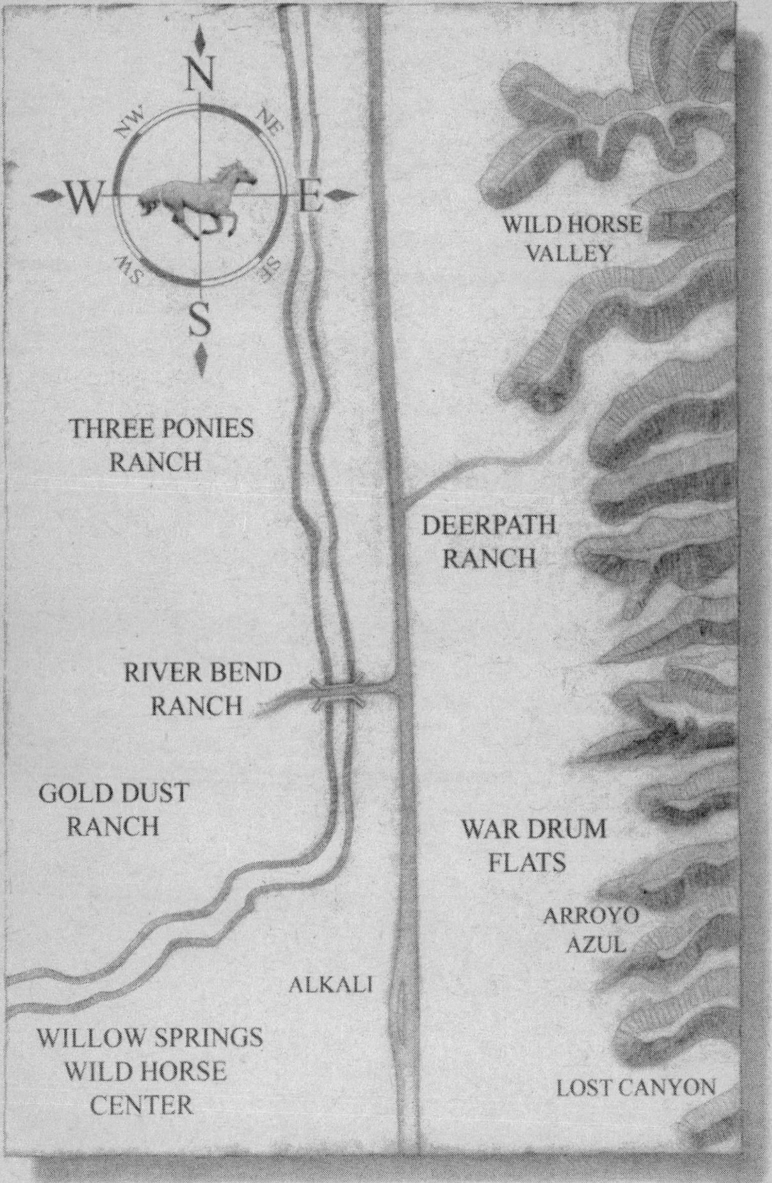
N
NW
NE
W
E
SW
SE
S
WILD HORSE VALLEY
THREE PONIES RANCH
DEERPATH RANCH
RIVER BEND RANCH
GOLD DUST RANCH
WAR DRUM FLATS
ARROYO AZUL
ALKALI
WILLOW SPRINGS WILD HORSE CENTER
LOST CANYON

Chapter One

Cold desert winds spun snow dust off the ground and into a white whirlwind that surrounded Samantha Forster and the bay mustang she rode. She pulled her fleece-lined coat up to her chin. The huge stone barn at Three Ponies Ranch had just come into view, and she aimed her horse for it.

Sam glanced at her watch. She wasn't late, but she hadn't passed any of the Ely brothers hurrying off to work. She didn't hear doors slamming, buckets clanking, or truck engines warming up in the thirty-degree morning. The ranch ahead lay oddly silent.

Sam hurried Ace out of his walk and into a jog as they passed Three Ponies' front pasture. For a second, the bay threw his head high and she heard him suck in the scent of frosty sagebrush. Then, the second stirring of her legs, or the December wind whooshing his tail forward to tickle his flanks, made Ace dance.

Hooves churning, the bay insisted he should break into a lope.

"Save it," Sam told her horse.

And when a stocky chocolate-colored gelding galloped toward them, then raced along his pasture fence and she *still* didn't let Ace break out of a jog, her bay mustang gave a little buck just to show Sam who was boss.

"Not you," she corrected him, but she settled more firmly into her saddle, just in case.

They were in the Elys' ranch yard now, and though Sam considered herself a good sport, there was no way she wanted to start the morning with a surprise rodeo performance for the Ely brothers and their parents.

"Awful quiet," Sam said to Ace as they passed five white hens digging in their toenails for better traction as they raced for their coop.

The flock was the only sign of life, though her friend Jake should have had his mare Witch loaded in a horse trailer, ready to go. Sam had expected Jake to be leaning against the trailer, arms crossed with his Stetson tipped over his eyes, waiting impatiently for her to get here.

Scanning the ranch yard once more, Sam spotted

Gal, the Elys' German shepherd, digging at the bottom of the barn door.

Of course, Sam thought, smiling. Jake must be inside. She'd bet he hadn't been able to resist a few more minutes of play with Singer, his coydog pup.

She didn't blame him. After all, Singer was the reason Sam had ridden over to Three Ponies Ranch instead of waiting for Jake to pick her up on his way to Willow Springs Wild Horse Center.

Sam heard the empty porch swing creak as the wind pushed it to the limit of its chains. And then a door slammed. Twisting in her saddle, Sam saw she was wrong about Jake. He wasn't in the barn, because here he came.

Wide-shouldered and purposeful, Jake strode toward her.

Sensing her distraction, Ace snorted, turned to face Jake, and Sam let him. Her mouth had already opened on a greeting when Jake jerked his black Stetson toward the hitching rack in a wordless sign that she should tie Ace and dismount.

From someone else, the gesture might have been rude, but not from Jake. Western movie characters who were "strong, silent types" could easily have been based on cowboys like him.

As Sam slung Ace's reins over the hitching rail, Jake came to stand beside her.

"Good morning," she said. "It's almost Christmas."

Sam knew she could wait all day for Jake to join

her excitement. After all, she hadn't asked him a question, had she?

Sam bent, loosened Ace's cinch, and heard her horse groan with relief. Just when she was thinking her horse was a better communicator than Jake, he spoke up.

"You're just in time to welcome back everybody's hero."

Sam straightened to face Jake.

"Huh?" she asked, rubbing her chilled hands together.

"Kit's coming home today," he said.

"Kit?" Sam gasped. "Really?"

Kit was the oldest of the six Ely brothers, the one she barely remembered. He'd left to follow the rodeo circuit just after graduating from high school. Though he rarely came home, most folks in the area followed Kit's career.

Last summer, it had been big news when Bryan Ely had mentioned Kit's purchase of a new red truck with his rodeo winnings. Before that, Clara had taped a clipping from "Rodeo Today" to her coffee shop cash register because it showed Kit Ely riding a blue roan bucking horse named No-No Nitro.

If the rumors Sam had heard were true, Kit was headed for the national finals in bronc riding.

Jake was right. Kit was definitely a local hero.

"Wow, you mean he's home for Christmas?" Sam asked.

"He will be," Jake said. "He called at about midnight. Don't know if Mom even slept. She was up before daylight makin' cinnamon rolls. Adam called in and took the day off from his kayak guide job in Reno. Bryan and Quinn are waitin' to go out and evict that deer herd from the timothy hay field." Jake shook his head over his brothers. "Dad's goin' in late to work and even Nate stayed home, and he's got some big paper due that he was gonna go in and research at the library."

As Jake glanced back at the river rock ranch house, Sam figured six of the eight members of the Ely family were probably sitting around the kitchen table, out of the icy winds.

"You want to go back in?" Sam asked, in case Jake had left the rest of his family to come meet her.

"No, but Mom said she'd wring my neck if I leave before Kit gets here. So, you might as well give Singer some time while I work the kinks out of Witch. You mind?"

"Of course not," Sam said.

She looked after Jake as he went to catch his mare, Witch. Maybe it was just the squabble with his mother that was keeping Jake outside, but Sam didn't think so. And there was something else she wanted to ask him.

It seemed like she'd heard the championship rodeo was nicknamed "Cowboy Christmas," because contestants could win huge prizes. Wasn't it held about now? Eight hundred miles away in Las Vegas? So why would Kit be coming home, now?

Sam didn't ask. She didn't try to get Jake to explain what was bothering him, either. Jake had been her friend since they were little kids and though he was more comfortable with horses than people, over the years she'd learned to read his silences pretty well.

If she stayed alert, she'd figure out what it was about Kit's return that made Jake act annoyed instead of excited.

The Elys' dog Gal was still whining when Sam reached the barn. The dog butted her nose at the space where the barn doors rattled against their bolts as the wind fought to snatch them open.

Sam laughed at the dog's determination as Gal tried to squeeze 130 pounds of German shepherd through a slot barely wide enough for a mouse.

But Sam knew why Gal was trying so hard. Singer, Jake's coydog, was making high-pitched yaps, begging the big dog to come play.

The pup was irresistible to Sam, too. Because of Singer, she'd been to Three Ponies Ranch more in the past three weeks than she had in the last two years. She adored her dog Blaze's half-wild pup, but it hadn't been hard to give him up. From the moment she'd seen Singer mirrored in Jake's eyes, she'd known the two belonged together.

Not that it was easy raising a little creature with warring natures.

Jake insisted the coydog had to socialize with

outsiders to his Three Ponies territory, so he'd had Sam work with the pup as much as she could.

"And I feel like a real outsider today," Sam muttered to Gal as she worked to loosen the barn door bolt. "I don't belong in the middle of a family reunion."

The German shepherd gazed up at Sam with confused eyes, then pawed with renewed energy at the base of the doors.

"Okay, okay," Sam told the dog.

The bolt slid free. As Sam eased inside, she almost tripped over Gal.

By the time Sam closed the door behind them so that Singer couldn't escape, the dogs had bowed in tail-wagging greeting to each other.

"You lucky dog," Sam told Singer as he bounced away from Gal and jumped high enough to lick Sam's nose. "It's warmer in here than it is in my bedroom!"

Three Ponies Ranch had been a cavalry post during the Civil War, and the main house, barn, and a small structure the Elys called "the little house" were built with walls that were two feet thick to withstand attack by hostile Indians.

And that, Sam thought, smiling, was kind of ironic, since Jake's dad Luke was a full-blooded Shoshone.

Singer and Gal didn't care about any of that, as they raced around the barn in crazy circles. Openmouthed and agile, Singer bounded over hay bales, then ran with his head low enough to snap at Gal's paws. When the big dog swung around to face him, Singer gave a surprised bark. But he darted aside, easily dodging Gal's charge.

While the dogs played, Sam took Singer's light leather harness from a nail. Singer had slipped his head out of every collar that wasn't tight enough to choke him, and he couldn't be trusted to stay nearby on his own, so the harness and long leash was a compromise to keep him safe. After all, his mother had been shot for venturing too close to civilization.

When Singer's gray-brown ears caught the jingle of a buckle on the harness, the coydog stopped. Panting and alert, he trotted away from Gal and bumped against Sam's legs.

Gal threw herself belly down in the straw, watching as the pup ducked his head into the harness and Sam clicked the buckles closed around his body.

"Good boy," Sam said, rubbing her hands all over the pup.

Singer laid his ears back and made a worried sound, but he knew this was the price he paid for time outside, and Jake had convinced Sam that constant handling would help Singer listen to his tame nature instead of his wild one.

"Let's go," Sam said, shouldering the barn door open.

Singer gave Gal a single backward glance before following Sam into the wind, but they'd only run a few steps when the pup stopped to watch his master.

Jake had brought the blue Scout truck, which he shared with his brothers, into the middle of the ranch yard. He'd loaded Ace into the horse trailer and now, loose in the saddle, Jake showed the ease of a lifelong horseman as he rode out his black mare's irritation.

Jake squinted at a flapping roof shingle that the winds had peeled up on the bunkhouse while his heels and hands dealt with Witch's fuss.

Sam hunched her shoulders inside her jacket. This morning, the thermometer on her front porch at River Bend Ranch had stayed stubbornly below freezing when Sam thumped it. Winds like these usually blew in late afternoon. Jake's horse, Witch, seemed to know it.

Jake turned the horse's tail to the gusts and waited for her to hump up her back and buck.

While Sam had done all she could to keep Ace from bucking this morning, Jake seemed eager for it. But Witch didn't look serious about pitching Jake off her back. She just seemed grouchy either because Jake had hurried her through breakfast or because she'd spotted the horse trailer with Ace already inside and figured, rightly, that it was waiting for her.

Hands easy on the reins, Jake swayed with Witch's movements. Tilting his chin toward his chest, Jake coaxed the mare into loping figure eights. His hair was finally growing out, and Sam saw the ends of it gleaming blue-black beneath his Stetson.

The wind's sudden blast broke Singer's concentration. He wrapped the leash around Sam's knees and gave a bunch of excited yaps. While she settled him down, Sam thought she heard something.

Could it be Kit?

Over the wind's screech, Sam listened for an approaching truck. She kind of wished Kit would hurry.

But it wasn't an engine's roar that soared above the wind. There was a sudden crack. A branch snapped off a cottonwood tree as if a giant hand had swatted it down.

Ace's hooves drummed inside the horse trailer and Witch shied. Jake ducked as the branch blew past, but it was still airborne, bobbing as if it were carried by an invisible wave, when Jake wheeled Witch toward the naked branch, making her face what she feared.

But the branch didn't hit the ground. It struck the windshield of Jake's truck and broke it.

Like silent lightning, a zigzag crazed the glass.

Singer cringed at the sound, then stood barking.

"Shh," Sam said, petting the pup into silence.

Suddenly, as if she had to show up the misbehaving pup, Witch gave a sigh and stood calmly. As soon as Jake cued her to approach the horse trailer, she did it.

Jake's right boot had lifted from his stirrup and nearly cleared Witch's back when the mare shied again, hard enough that Sam actually heard Jake's teeth crack together.

"Oops," Sam said, but then Gal rushed up beside her and Singer lunged to the end of the leash.

Light-bodied but quick, he didn't manage to jerk the leash from Sam's hand, but his leap surprised her.

All three animals had sensed something, and this time it wasn't the wind.

Sam glanced at Jake to see what he thought, but his attention was focused on Witch. His leg came on over the mare's back and he stayed balanced on his left stirrup.

Only after he planted both boots on the ground did Jake stare in the direction in which the mare's ears pointed.

Through a thin veil of blowing snow, Sam made out a stranger coming down the road. He had a saddle balanced on one shoulder and the fringe on his leather chinks flapped out like raven's wings.

With a single woof, Gal bounded out of the barn, past Sam and Singer, and stopped next to Jake.

The dog leaned against his leg before she raised her black nose. Sniffing, she searched the wind for more than sagebrush and horses for a full minute before her tail curled over her back, wagging.

"It must be someone she knows," Sam told Singer when the pup whined.

As Gal catapulted toward the front gate, barking, the ranch house door slammed open. Maxine and

Luke Ely, Nate, Adam, Quinn, and Bryan all came out smiling.

"Kit," Jake said to himself.

Sam wouldn't have heard him if she hadn't been standing so close, and Jake's wondering tone made her feel shy. She tugged Singer away from Jake and his family, and she didn't stop until they reached the stone barn. She squatted next to the pup, away from the action, and hoped she'd be invisible.

All the Elys jockeyed for a look at Kit as he came closer.

Even though they blocked her view of Kit, Sam saw Jake wrap a single rein around his hand. Was he worried Witch, too, would run toward his oldest brother?

Kit was just steps away when Sam got her first glimpse of him. His smile hit her first.

Surrounded by his family, Kit grinned like a happy wolf. He looked older than Sam thought he would. The wrinkles raying around his eyes must have been from the sunny glare of hundreds of rodeo arenas or the miles of highway that linked them together.

But why was Kit afoot? Where was the new red truck Bryan had mentioned?

Sam squinted to make out the letters on the tooled leather saddle Kit carried on his shoulder.

ALL AROUND COWBOY . . .

Wow. She couldn't read *where* Kit had earned the

trophy saddle, but it had a suede seat and fancy stitching, and it shone like the mahogany table Gram polished with lemon oil. The saddle was almost too pretty to ride.

Everybody's hero, Jake had called his big brother, and Sam could see why. Though Jake had said the words in a teasing way, she knew Kit had done things Jake aspired to.

Kit even *looked* like an Indian cowboy should. His fresh-pressed shirt was the color of oatmeal and cream, and some kind of blue stones were strung on a leather thong around his neck. He strode toward his family with the stiff grace of a man who'd ridden his share of rough stock.

Champion bronc rider Kit Ely didn't look cocky, though. He looked proud. If he hadn't been twenty-five–or–whatever years old, Sam imagined every girl at Darton High School, including her, could develop a crush on him.

"Where's your truck?" Bryan asked.

Sam wondered why his dad sent Bryan such a cold look. She'd been asking herself the same thing.

"Traveling light," Kit said.

He dipped his right shoulder to maneuver the saddle to the ground and Sam noticed Kit's left forearm was encased in a cast. Maybe he hadn't just come home for Christmas, she thought.

She stole a quick glance at Jake, to see if he'd noticed, but his back was to her.

Once Kit had settled the saddle, he made a faint movement that seemed to launch his family's welcome.

Mrs. Ely flew forward first. She looked suddenly blonder and smaller. She couldn't reach around his neck, so Kit bent to meet her. Her embrace knocked off his hat, and then she was crying against his shoulder, giving him so much more than a hug, Sam had to look away.

She guessed it didn't matter how many kids you had, every one was special. Kit's wandering ways obviously hadn't been easy on his mother.

Sam heard Jake clear his throat. Did his throat feel like hers—so stiff she might have swallowed a stick? Sam still couldn't see Jake's face, but he hung a thumb in one pocket and shook his head, pretending not to be touched.

"Mom's losin' it," Quinn said, sounding as uncomfortable as Jake looked, but their dad's hand made a slice through the air that told Quinn to shut up.

Trembling and attentive, Singer pressed his shoulder against Sam's.

The pup's black-dot eyebrows shifted up and down, and Sam whispered to Singer to distract him.

"Maybe Kit let a friend borrow his truck. Maybe he can't drive with that cast."

Kit had said he was traveling light, and he meant it. He carried nothing except a gray duffle bag and the saddle.

Somebody must have dropped him off, though, Sam thought. Walking any distance in those chinks couldn't be comfortable.

"Honey, what happened to your arm?" Mrs. Ely asked, one hand hovering above the cast.

"It's nothing," Kit said. "Comes with the territory. You know."

Shaking her head, Mrs. Ely let her son shrug free. Luke Ely clapped his son on the shoulder. Next, Nate, Adam, Bryan, and Quinn were pounding their big brother on the back and shaking his hand.

Why didn't Jake get in there, too? Sam wondered. Even Gal, yodeling for attention, got a scratch behind the ears before Kit noticed Jake.

"Baby Bear," Kit greeted him, but then, Sam saw him look Jake over and shake his head.

Baby Bear? Sam winced. Jake would hate that. But then she saw Kit's eyes measure Jake.

Kit gave a short laugh. "Not anymore, I guess. You're tall as me. How'd that happen?"

Jake still didn't say a thing.

"Gosh, Jake," Sam whispered in disgust.

But Kit didn't look hurt. He just changed the subject.

"Witch is lookin' good." Kit patted the mare's shoulder.

Ears pinned and teeth bared, Witch's head swung around to glare at Kit. Finally Jake turned sideways and Sam saw his face.

She expected him to keep the mare from confronting Kit, but Jake didn't even scold her.

Sam thought maybe she was wrong, but it almost looked like Jake was testing his big brother.

Chapter Two

If Jake had been testing his big brother's skill with horses, Kit passed.

He didn't say a word, simply inclined his head and stared Witch down.

The mare closed her mouth, shivered her skin as if she'd only been reacting to a fly, then gazed off toward the Calico Mountains.

Sam was delighted by Kit's performance, but it was weird sitting here, watching all this. The Elys had clearly forgotten all about her. Even Jake didn't seem to recall she was over by the barn with Singer, watching their family reunion as if she had a front-row seat at a play.

But what was she supposed to do? Jump up and

push her way into the middle of things? That would be ruder than eavesdropping. Wouldn't it?

Besides, she and her best friend Jen had always wondered about the oldest, wandering Ely brother.

"So far, the guy is amazing," Sam whispered to Singer, but the coydog didn't act impressed. Instead of lifting his head from his paws, he closed his eyelids more tightly.

"Where you all going?" Kit asked, noticing the open horse trailer with Ace inside.

"Nowhere," Nate said, but his response overlapped Jake's.

"Willow Springs," Jake said, and when a corner of Kit's mouth twitched as if the name meant nothing to him, Jake added, "The BLM corrals." He nodded south. "Mustang auction coming up."

"Jake's going to herd horses from the far pens, up closer to the BLM offices, so potential adopters can get a better look at them," Mrs. Ely explained.

"How'd an Ely come to be working for the BLM?" Kit's amazement reminded Sam that practically no ranchers—or their sons, apparently—appreciated the Bureau of Land Management.

"For Brynna Forster," Mrs. Ely said, but Jake corrected her.

"For a pretty good wage."

Kit gave a short laugh. "I hear ya. But who's *Brynna* Forster? I remember the little girl, but that wasn't her name."

Sam's cheeks burned with a blush. If she was going to be brave enough to jump up and introduce herself, this was her cue to do it.

"You're thinkin' of Samantha," Quinn said. "She's fourteen."

"And she's around here somewhere," Adam said, glancing around the ranch yard.

Sam felt that awful exposed feeling she remembered from playing hide-and-seek as a little kid. She'd never been good at finding hiding places. Apparently she still wasn't.

Jake looked straight at Sam, then beckoned her to leave the shadow of the barn and come on over.

Feeling more awkward by the second, Sam stalled. She held up a finger to signal she'd be right back, then slipped inside the barn and released Singer with an apology for not taking him on a longer walk.

Then, she drew a deep breath, bolted the barn doors, and headed toward the Elys.

Coming closer, she heard Kit say, "Fourteen? Can't be."

"You've been gone most of the last five years," Mrs. Ely said reproachfully, but then she seemed to hear how she was scolding her grown-up son and her tone turned cheery again. "Half the state's followed your career."

Kit rubbed the back of his neck in a gesture identical to one Jake used whenever he felt uneasy, and Sam smiled.

"Here comes Sam," Quinn announced.

Although she didn't think of herself as shy, the burden of all those eyes fixed on her made Sam wish Quinn had kept quiet.

Get a grip, Sam told herself. Then she not only stood taller, she swept her auburn hair behind her ears and smiled.

Kit's head moved in a slow shake of denial. "Can't be," he said again.

Sam looked to Jake for help, but his eyes were fixed on Witch.

Luckily, his dad noticed Sam's uneasiness and broke in.

"Now, before you go telling Samantha you haven't seen her since she was knee high to a grasshopper," Luke Ely joked, "let's go on inside and eat the breakfast your mom's been making since dawn."

"Not me," Jake said, then turned to his mother. "Sorry."

"You've got ten minutes before you have to leave," Mrs. Ely said in her no-nonsense teacher tone. Then she fluttered her hands at her sons, herding them back inside.

As an only child, Sam enjoyed the noisy, affectionate joking that made breakfast with the Elys practically a party, even though it didn't last long.

Ten minutes wasn't enough time to describe all the prize money and bruises Kit had earned since his last visit home. It wasn't enough time to list the states he'd slept in or describe the small-town arenas and big-city event centers with instant-replay screens that would dwarf the kitchen wall. But Kit tried, and he squeezed in enough excitement that he left Sam's head spinning.

Pushing back from the table, Jake glanced at his mother. She nodded that he could leave, but Sam was surprised when Kit looked at his mom in the same way, as if he wanted permission to leave, too.

Adam must have missed it completely, because he asked, "Kit, wanna ride out with us?"

"Take a look at the old home place?" Bryan teased.

"The parts the white-tails have left us," Quinn, the second youngest, tried to sound gruff as he mentioned the deer that had been grazing in the hay field.

"I'll ride along with Baby Bear, if he don't mind."

Jake flinched as hard at the nickname as Mrs. Ely did from Kit's bad grammar.

"Doesn't," Mrs. Ely corrected.

"Like bein' a kid again," Kit said, grinning. Then he turned to Jake and waited for an answer.

"Fine," Jake said.

He didn't add, *As long as you don't call me Baby Bear again,* but Sam would bet he was thinking it.

Having Kit come with them to Willow Springs would be fun, Sam thought as Jake led the way out, but Jake and Kit were both tall and broad-shouldered.

It would be a pretty crowded ride.

Sam crossed her fingers, hoping Witch wouldn't pull some trick to make Jake look bad in front of his big brother, but when he led the mare toward the trailer, she behaved like there was a bushel of carrots waiting inside.

"Easy loader," Kit said as Witch ambled up the ramp.

Jake looked down, hiding his smile, and Sam knew Kit's approval pleased him. As Jake pulled the truck keys from his pocket, he glanced at Kit.

"You drive," Kit said, "and Samantha, why don't you sit in the middle and be the rose between the thorns?"

"Okay," she said, laughing, but then she saw Jake evaluating her reaction.

Maybe he was just disgruntled, since he grabbed and flung away the branch that had broken his windshield at about the same time Kit had arrived. Just the same, Sam felt her lips lose their smile.

Sitting elbow to elbow with the Ely brothers wasn't comfy, but she thought it was kind of nice that Kit didn't mention the newly cracked windshield or the way he had to lay his cast across his lap. He just leaned back in the passenger's seat with a groan.

"Y'okay?" Jake asked.

"As much as I ever am," Kit said.

"Your arm?" Sam asked, but Kit shook his head and lifted his necklace so she and Jake could see chunks of brown-streaked turquoise cut into rough beads.

"Notice how all of 'em slide on the string and jam together? That's what my vertebrae do every time I draw a sunfishing bronc."

Sam shuddered, imagined herself astride a bucking horse that alternately dove for the dirt, then slammed up into a sky-pawing rear.

"Bet that's hard to get used to," Jake said as he turned the key in the truck's ignition.

The words were barely sympathetic, but Sam heard his admiration for Kit's grit.

"You got that right," Kit said, then sighed. "If you'll pardon me, Samantha," he said, tilting his hat down over his eyes, "it's nap time."

"Sure," Sam said, but she gave Jake a sidelong glance, kind of wondering why Kit needed a nap so early in the morning.

Jake ignored Sam's silent question.

They drove away from Three Ponies, taking a dirt road to the highway along the La Charla River, past the turnoff to River Bend.

Just minutes after Sam thought Kit was dozing, he spoke up again.

"I've walked down lots of roads at night, but I could tell this one led home. Only saw a single truck on the highway. Even though it had a burned-out headlight, it blinked the other one hello."

Sam smiled at the small-town courtesy. If that

happened to you on a deserted street in San Francisco, you'd be a little worried over what it meant.

"Huh," Jake said.

After that, Kit slept without moving, even when the pavement ended and the road up to Willow Springs turned to rock-hard corduroy.

Sam wondered if she should tell Jake and Kit to expect more uneasiness when they reached Willow Springs. Her stepmother Brynna, manager of the BLM's wild horse corrals, was finding it difficult to get along with Norman White. The man had been hired to take her place as soon as she left on maternity leave, and they were clashing because he'd shown up early.

It had been Norman's idea to have this unscheduled wild horse adoption event, and it was just the kind of crazy decision that made Brynna put off the start date of her leave so that Norman could do as little damage as possible to the captive wild horses.

Sam sighed. Loudly. But Jake gave no sign he'd welcome a little conversation. Sam was pretty sure whispers wouldn't wake Kit, but Jake kept his eyes focused on the road, and he was frowning.

Twisting as far as she could without bumping either Ely, Sam looked out the window behind her head. She could see a wisp of Ace's black mane inside the trailer and she couldn't help thinking what she always did: Her bay gelding was better to have a talk with than Jake.

It wasn't until the road slanted up through Thread the Needle, where there was barely enough room for a single car to pass between the cliffs, that Kit awakened.

"Passin' through Alkali, I stopped for a cup of coffee," Kit said, resuming his earlier conversation with Jake as if he hadn't slept in the middle of it. "Sittin' at the counter, I overheard someone sayin' you're the real horseman of the family now—"

"Who said that?" Jake snapped out the question, but Kit didn't answer, didn't push his hat brim up, didn't even seem to hear.

"Maybe we'll have to get us a couple wild horses, little brother, and see if you can prove it."

Chapter Three

He had to be joshing with Jake, Sam thought, looking between the two.

Kit's remark surely hadn't been a dare, because he just dropped the idea as he climbed out of the truck and took a look around at Willow Springs Wild Horse Center.

"Ain't this a sorry setup?" Kit asked, as he offered Sam a hand getting down.

Sam gave a tight smile and hopped down on her own. Then she surveyed the BLM facility, trying to see it as Kit did.

She saw acres of pipe corrals filled with horses, a wall of hay bales twice as tall as her home, an office building, and a parking lot with white trucks labeled

U.S. GOVERNMENT. This morning's light snow had melted off, leaving mud in low places, but the footing inside the corrals had been designed so that the moisture ran off and the horses weren't standing in puddles.

Brynna worked hard here and so did Hugh and Brynna's secretary, her two permanent staff members. Half of Sam wanted to ask Kit to explain what was "sorry" about it, but she already knew.

Kit was a cowboy. He would protest that the wild horses grazing on his family's ranch were competing for the grass that cattle grew fat on. Still, he looked as disappointed as she'd felt on her first visit here. Sam knew it was because of the horses.

The pipe corrals were filled with mustangs. Mustangs were supposed to be running wild with blowing manes and tails, challenging humans to catch them, confronting each other in mock battles, and defying fences that imprisoned them. Here, nothing like that was happening. These horses looked dull and resigned to captivity.

That's what Kit thought was a sorry sight.

"Wait until you see wild horses trucked in fresh off the range," Sam said. "Or watch them being loaded into the trailers after the auction."

From the corner of her eye, Sam caught Jake's expression. There, then instantly gone, it had been a look of disbelief.

Mustangs looked wild and beautiful when they were fresh off the range or being loaded because they were terrified. Had she really been offering horses' panic as entertainment?

Sam was ashamed. She didn't know what to say.

"Am I ever glad to see some friendly faces." A female voice floated from the direction of the office. "I never would have let Hugh take time off, but he called me a grinch!"

Sam, Jake, and Kit turned to see Brynna approaching. In her khaki uniform and official nametag, Brynna still managed to look confident and very much the boss, though she was round with pregnancy.

Jake frowned, and Sam remembered how he'd steadied Brynna to keep her from falling the other day. It was pretty clear he thought she should begin her maternity leave now. In contrast, Kit grinned at Brynna as you would at a kitten.

"Brynna, this is Jake's brother Kit," Sam rushed to introduce them.

"The bronc rider," Brynna said with a nod. "Welcome." She extended her hand and clasped Kit's in a firm grip. "You've come to the right place if you'd like a horse to help with your homework." Her eyes swept the corrals of wild horses before halting on Kit's cast. Her lips pursed with interest, not pity. "Did a bronc do that?"

"Yep," Kit said. "It's nothing."

A faint alarm went off in Sam's mind. Twice she'd heard Kit dismiss the injury as "nothing." Knowing what she did about cowboys, she wasn't convinced. She'd been with Jake when he'd broken his leg in a riding accident. It had been a compound fracture. The bone had actually stabbed through his skin, but Jake had dismissed the blood and pain and just asked her to find his hat and get it back on his head.

"Are you still riding?" Brynna asked.

"Takin' a little time off for the holidays," Kit answered.

"You probably deserve it, so I won't draft you to help Jake and Sam move the horses around. You can just watch them and"—Brynna's voice took on a wheedling tone—"shop for a new horse?"

"I might do that," Kit said.

At first Sam thought he was just being polite, but Kit's eyes drifted to the stallion corral. What if he *hadn't* been joshing with Jake when he suggested a wild horse showdown?

She'd have to worry about it later, because Brynna was rattling off instructions, telling her and Jake to make sure the foals and yearlings were in pens up close where people could see them, to check that the corrals were labeled according to the horses inside, and to make sure each animal had a red and white rope loop holding a number around its neck.

"And though I hate it, I guess you'd better make sure all the older horses—everyone over ten," she added with a grimace, "are moved out of the adoption corrals. I think that's already done, but Hugh left a few mature mares and a few burros from southern Nevada, and Norman figured it out."

"Why's that a problem, now?" Kit asked.

"Congress voted to pull horses over ten years old from the adoption program," Brynna began.

"That's right. I heard about that," Kit said, then paused next to a corral. "And these are the studs?"

"Yes, though they're not as feisty without mares to protect or show off for," Brynna said.

"That red boy's a beauty," Jake said, pointing at a bright bay stallion that was watching him with pricked ears.

Kit nodded. "Have you finished roundups for a while?"

Brynna made a hum of disapproval and her lips parted, but Kit rushed to explain.

"I'm thinking, if I were to get a wild one, I'd want to imprint him as soon as I could."

It was only a small movement. Jake's hands still hung at his sides, but when they tightened into fists, Sam wondered why.

"That's a good idea," Brynna said. She tucked a loose tendril of hair back into her French braid. When she spoke again, it was in a halting, stop-start manner that was totally unlike her. "We have lots of horses here, too many, really. . . ." Brynna shook her head. "I'd like to say we were finished with non-emergency gathers, but my associate . . ." She glanced toward the office. "Well, he has a different opinion."

Brynna's sigh lasted a long time. "Just keep in touch, Kit. If we bring in more horses, I'd love you to have one of them."

"That'd be a first for Three Ponies," Jake said.

"Then it's about time," Sam told him, and turned toward Kit. "Your timing couldn't be better, since everyone's so glad to see you. They're not going to say no!"

"Don't know about that," Kit said. "Comin' home for the holidays is one thing; moving back with two new mouths to feed is something else."

Jake looked down for a second and Sam saw his fists clinch tighter. She could tell Jake wanted to ask Kit which it was. Was he home for a visit or was he moving back for good? Sam didn't understand the tension between the brothers, but maybe part of it was not knowing what to expect.

It didn't take Sam and Jake long to do the herding Brynna had asked for, and Sam left Jake walking around the corrals, checking out horses with Kit while she slung Ace's reins around a hitching rail and walked toward Brynna's office.

It was quiet except for the hum of a computer.

Sam slipped into the office unnoticed. The scent of dust and horses clung to her and she was about to walk back to Brynna's office and slip into the restroom to wash up when she heard voices raised in an argument.

At first Brynna's words didn't sink in, because her stepmother's tone trembled on the brink of angry tears. That was totally out of character for Brynna at work.

". . . not my last day . . ."

Of course it wasn't, Sam thought. Brynna had extended her work time when she discovered Norman White was her replacement.

"That was an informal request." Norman White's voice was level, but there was a gloating quality to it that Sam knew she wasn't imagining. "And of course you're welcome to stay on, but my wage as your replacement kicks in today."

Gooseflesh spread down Sam's arms. He was giving Brynna a choice. She could finish up today and leave, or continue to work, taking orders from him.

What would be the point? One more paycheck wasn't enough to keep Brynna working for a man who didn't know what he was doing, was it?

The silence stretched out until Sam wanted to burst into the other room, but she didn't. When Brynna spoke again, her voice was calmer.

"My regional supervisor approved my leave and amended the start date," Brynna pointed out.

"I'm sure he did, but I'm just following regulations, and my most recent communications with Washington, D.C., say that I begin work as director of Willow Springs Wild Horse Center at one minute after midnight, tonight."

"Norman, I took my boss at his word," Brynna said, and Sam heard her shuffling papers now, as if this conversation was merely a nuisance. "I'll go on leave in two weeks, not tomorrow. I have work to finish up."

Neither Brynna nor Norman were admitting their real motives for being in charge. Norman said he was just following regulations. Brynna said she had too much work to leave now. In fact, each thought the other was dead wrong in their method of running Willow Springs.

In this second silence, Sam heard a crackling sound. A nearly empty carafe had been left in the coffee maker. It was still turned on and the quarter-inch of brown liquid was baking. Sam would have rushed to turn it off if Norman hadn't started talking again.

"It's time to give yourself a break, Brynna. This job is getting too personal for you."

"I'm not sure I understand what you mean," Brynna said. The paper shuffling stopped, but her tone stayed cool as she added, "Could you give me an example?"

"We could begin with your bias *against* Linc Slocum and *in favor* of that gray stallion in the Calico Mountains," Norman said.

"Linc Slocum's applications have been denied because of two documented violations of the harassment and negligence clauses in the 1971 Free-Roaming Wild Horse and Burro Act. I can print you a copy of those regulations," Brynna offered.

Sam wanted to applaud until Norman corrected Brynna.

"You know that law was revised. It's in limbo now. And when I checked your files, I saw an awful lot of notes on pretty purple paper. Using a cheat sheet from your teenage stepdaughter kind of escalates your treatment of Mr. Slocum to a vendetta."

They *were* Sam's notes, but she'd done her research in online government documents. Maybe the purple paper had been a mistake, Sam thought, but he couldn't deny what she'd written was accurate.

"Norman, are you aware of the other charges pending against Slocum?"

"The uproar over that Gypsy boy?" Norman said carelessly. "That's not part of our evaluation process and, well . . ." He gave a humorless chuckle. "You might not want to put yourself into the position of the pot calling the kettle black."

"I don't follow you, Norman." Brynna's voice grew quieter and something in her tone reminded Sam of the day she'd seen Brynna strap on her service revolver and tug on a drab olive SWAT team cap to go after horse rustlers.

"I mean," Norman's voice rose as if he were struggling for patience, "you should have either brought in that feral gray stallion—for crying out loud, everyone knows he was bred and born on your husband's ranch—and paid the trespass fees going back four years to the time of his escape, or put him up for adoption."

"There's BLM precedent for releasing horses that could improve herd bloodlines," Brynna said.

"Sure, that's the reason you stated, but the horse is a troublemaker, and you were only thinking—"

"Thank goodness you're here to explain what I was thinking," Brynna cracked, but Norman didn't swerve from his tirade.

"You only left him on the range because he's a personal pet of your stepdaughter's who thinks the notion of private horses running free on public land is romantic and stirs the soul."

"Your timeline's a little out of sync, Norman. Samantha wasn't my stepdaughter when that determination was made."

"Exactly." Norman broke the word into three distinct syllables. He sounded as if he believed he'd sprung a trap.

"Once more, I'm afraid you're going to have to spell out what you're thinking," Brynna said, "because I'm not following you."

For a minute it was so quiet, Sam hoped Norman had really heard himself and figured out that he'd overstepped his prized professionalism.

"Just what are you implying?" Brynna asked.

"Certainly not that you used that gray to please Samantha and catch Wyatt's attention."

"That's ridiculous," Brynna said.

"I agree. I'm certain your emotional instability is more recent, linked to hormones and your pregnancy."

Emotional instability?

Sam waited. She couldn't imagine what Brynna would do next.

"Norman, I'll hang my decision on the BLM in Washington. I'll e-mail a request for clarification and proceed accordingly. In the meantime, we're just going to have to agree we have different approaches to this job."

A loud popping sound came from the overheated coffee carafe as it cracked. For an instant, Sam wondered at the coincidence of Jake's broken windshield and the broken coffeepot. But either Brynna or Norman were bound to come investigate the sound, and Sam didn't want to be caught sitting there, eavesdropping, when that happened.

She tiptoed quickly to the door and slipped outside, unseen, but Brynna's voice rose so sharply from inside that she heard her ask, "What's that sound?"

Cracking coffeepot? Tiptoeing boots?

No. Something throbbed from overhead, compelling Sam to look up into the icy blue sky. She saw a glint of metal.

"Norman?" Brynna asked.

"It's a chopper."

"A chopper?"

"One of our contract pilots is doing a flyover of

canyons and valleys."

Sam stared up, watching the helicopter's rotor blades flash silver, gold, and silver again.

"It's just an observation," Norman told Brynna stiffly. "For now."

Chapter Four

If Kit and Jake continued their sibling rivalry while driving her home to River Bend Ranch, Sam didn't notice.

Once she'd loaded Ace into the trailer beside Witch, she thought of nothing but the conversation she'd overheard between Brynna and Norman White. As if her mind hid a tape recorder, she played it over and over again, studying each word for tone and hidden meaning.

She'd been confused by Brynna's attitude when she'd come out of her office to have Sam and Jake sign the paperwork that would result in them getting paid for their two hours of work. Bustling and looking as capable and calm as ever, Brynna was either a really good actress, or she was confident the BLM would keep her on so that she could supervise Norman White for two more weeks.

Brynna's feelings had to be hurt, Sam thought, as Jake steered the Scout through Thread the Needle, headed for the highway. Trained as a biologist and long respected in a traditionally male job, Brynna prized her reputation for logic and levelheadedness. Being called emotionally unstable was a stinging insult.

And Norman White must be convinced the BLM would come down on his side, or he wouldn't have a helicopter pilot searching canyons and valleys. Sooner or later, he'd do another gather, and his comments about the Phantom made it clear which herd area he'd start in.

Together, Jake and Kit turned their heads to stare at her. Had she given a heavy sigh or made some squeak of distress? Sam didn't know, but she made an excuse, anyway.

"I was kind of dozing," she said. The excuse didn't make much sense, but she couldn't tell them about a conversation she shouldn't have even heard.

"Ticked off at old Norman?" Jake asked.

"Of course!" Sam blurted. "He wants to take more mustangs off the range, but all he knows about is numbers. What's the average age and number of horses in a bachelor band? What's the foal production rate of a mustang mare and the correlation between that and how many mouthfuls of food she's had?"

The explosion of words surprised Sam. She wasn't very good at keeping her emotions inside when she was around Jake. Even having Kit for an audience didn't seem to work.

"Sorry," she apologized to Kit.

The older Ely brother lifted his shoulders in a shrug, then asked, "Aren't those things good to know if you're deciding to bring horses in?"

The question stopped the whirling of Sam's mind.

"They are," she admitted, "but he's—" Sam broke off and stared at the faded knees of her jeans, trying to think of a way to explain. "He doesn't feel anything about them. It's like, he doesn't even know they're living things. To him they might as well be"—Sam searched her mind for an example—"like checkers, and he's just trying to get as many as he can so that the board is empty."

"No heart," Jake told Kit. Sam couldn't tell what the faint smile on his lips meant until he added, "Bet he's aiming to round up your favorite wild bunch."

"How did you know?" Sam asked.

"Chopper," Jake said. "And it takes more to get you stirred up than it used to, 'cept when it comes to that gray stud."

Kit made an interested sound. Jake gave a quick shake of his head, but Sam's mind veered away from both of them.

What if Norman White convinced the federal government to bring in the Phantom and his herd? How could she save her horse?

"Wouldn't mind seein' one of our wild bunches. It's been a while," Kit said to Jake. "Don't suppose you know where you could scare one up on such short notice?"

Sam didn't hear a challenge in Kit's words, but once more, Jake did. Abruptly, he steered off the highway to follow a bumpy trail, then took a series of back roads—left, another left, and then right, to cut across a swampy spot. Sam was surprised Jake tried it with the horse trailer. She guessed he knew what he was doing, but by the time he stopped, somewhere behind River Bend Ranch and Three Ponies, near their shared boundary, she felt queasy.

"I've got to get out for a—" Sam broke off. She'd been about to admit she was feeling carsick. Alone with Jake that might have been okay, but it wasn't with Kit sitting there. "I'd like to get out and stretch my legs for a minute."

Kit bailed out of the Scout, grimacing as he used his other hand to balance his cast.

Sam walked away from the brothers to stare across an open plain that unrolled toward a column of gray granite backlit by a pale winter sun. It was Snakehead Peak.

In the trailer behind her, Ace and Witch shifted. Sam heard a faint rumble of faraway thunder.

"Forgot how sudden it can go cold here," Kit complained. "Has me thinking fond thoughts about rodeoin' in Arizona."

This spot was pretty in spring. Sam remembered antelope and wild horses grazing together here. Now, the cold breeze felt ominous.

Cloud shadows moved over the sagebrush and what was left of the bunch grass. Sam let her eyes unfocus, searching for movement. She wished she would see the Phantom.

"Most days they take a doze by that brush," Jake was telling Kit. "But this change in weather's got 'em worried."

Sam searched for the brush Jake was talking about, but she didn't spot it or the mustangs until a breeze set their manes blowing.

There! The herd stood with their tails to the wind, eating voraciously, snapping at band members who wandered too close.

Winter was here. Snow scented the wind and the mustangs concentrated on gobbling all the calories they could hold before seeking shelter.

Only the Phantom wasn't eating. He'd frozen to attention, eyes staring across at Sam.

The stallion stepped away from the other horses. His sudden move made the herd look up in alarm. Keeping his head higher than the others', the stallion neighed just as the clouds let a sunbeam pass through.

"How 'bout that?" Kit muttered.

Alone, Sam would have gone to the stallion, but now she just watched.

His ears tilted forward and his neck arched. A gleaming streak, bright as molten metal, followed its curve. Chin tucked, he bobbed his head, nodding an equine assurance Sam didn't understand, just before crosswinds caught his mane, tail, and forelock and he was surrounded with a corona of silver.

Sam heard Kit catch his breath as the Phantom pranced in place, showing off for her, though his herd returned to grazing. Then the stallion lowered his head, thrusting his muzzle in her direction before jerking his head to one side.

She was the only one in the world who knew what he was doing. If she'd been close enough, the stallion would have lowered his head beneath her arm, encouraging her to come for a ride. He pawed then, teasing her until Jake and Kit moved closer.

Then the Phantom's ears flattened. He burst into a contained gallop, making a circling rush around his band.

In moments, he'd arrived back exactly where he'd been, staring across the open space at the humans. He pawed the ground in four rapid, striking movements and his possessive snort carried to them.

Mine, he seemed to say. He waited for them to make the next move—if they dared.

Wordlessly, Jake and Kit began backing toward

the Scout, and Sam decided she should join them.

You win, boy, Sam thought, but she couldn't tear her eyes away. As she backed away after the brothers, her heart reached out to the stallion, pulling the connection between them thinner with each step.

Zanzibar, she thought longingly, but she wanted him to graze, to stay strong for the cold winter ahead, and she knew he wouldn't lower his head to eat while they stood watching him.

When the Scout's door creaked open, Kit said, "Needs oil," and the spell was broken.

As soon as they were settled with seat belts fastened and Jake was driving away, Kit said, "The way he was dippin' his head and kind of bowing reminds me of Sittin' Bull—"

"Don't tell her that story." Jake shook his head in disgust.

"—and the dancing white stallion," Kit finished.

"I want to hear it," Sam said, shooting Jake a glare.

Just then, the Scout made a laboring sound and bogged down in the mud.

The interruption was awfully convenient, Sam thought, but when the tires spun uselessly, Sam knew enough to be quiet and let Jake concentrate. Getting stuck up here with the horse trailer, especially when Kit didn't have full use of his arms, would mean dirty work for her and Jake.

As soon as the tires hit the highway, Kit said, "I

know you've heard of Sitting Bull, the great chief and holy man of the Lakota Sioux."

"Sure," Sam said, ignoring Jake's groan.

"And you know that after his people were defeated, he joined Buffalo Bill's Wild West show and traveled all over the world, performing?" Kit went on.

Sam nodded. She'd always thought it was a sad fate for a great warrior.

"But that wasn't the end," Kit told her.

"You are so—" Jake began, but Sam stopped him.

"It wasn't?" she asked, and elbowed Jake gently. She didn't want him to crash the truck, but she didn't want him to barge into Kit's story, either.

"Oh, no. Not nearly the end," Kit assured Sam. Then, drawing a deep breath, he said, "Sitting Bull spent time with the silly circus partly because of—"

"Annie Oakley, Little Sure Shot," Sam blurted. "Isn't that what he called her?"

"That's one story," Jake grumped.

"That's not right?" Sam asked Kit, blushing.

"Our grandfather says the chief stayed because of the magnificent white stallion Buffalo Bill had Sitting Bull ride in the show."

"Ohhh," Sam sighed. The chills racing down her neck, past her elbows, to the tips of her fingers told her this was a far better version of the truth.

"In the Wild West show, there were wagon races, shooting matches, and a special act in which the chief starred. In it, a stagecoach was chased and surrounded by a band of shooting, screaming Indians."

Kit's sarcastic tone took nothing away from the picture in Sam's imagination.

"And then Sitting Bull, wearing bleached buckskins and bright feathers, galloped in on his white stallion. The war painted horse leaped and reared and ran amid the gunfire, and finally bowed to his delighted audience, which, truth be told, liked the horse lots better than the chief."

"Of course, Sitting Bull wasn't a Shoshone," Jake put in, and Sam laughed. Jake must have forgiven his brother for telling her the story, so maybe he'd gotten over whatever was bugging him before. She felt satisfied by that possibility as Kit went on.

"Time passed, and even while the show was in Europe, Sitting Bull heard of the unrest stirring among the tribes. Sitting Bull decided it was time to leave show business," Kit said. "As a parting gift, Buffalo Bill gave his old friend the white stallion."

"Or he might've stolen him," Jake joked. "Remember, he—"

"—wasn't a Shoshone," Kit finished with a chuckle. "Still, the old man returned to his people and urged them to resist the government's campaign of stamping out Indian languages, religion, and ways. When the final clash came—and some say it was an outright assassination—Sitting Bull was afoot. He was shot many times. And he died."

A crow rode the wind overhead and stayed silent,

except for his beating wings.

"The horse could have saved him, I bet," Sam said, but when Jake and Kit didn't respond, the chills came back again and Sam asked, "What happened to his white stallion? Did he try to go to Sitting Bull?"

Jake rolled his eyes as if that was an unbearably romantic notion, but Kit said, "Maybe. All I know is that the stallion heard the awful gunfire and started doing what he knew how to do. He escaped the place where the chief had left him tied, and charged toward the sound he remembered." Kit looked into Sam's face as he added, "The sound of rifles."

Sam shivered.

"And then the stallion pranced," Kit said. "He leaped over bodies, untouched by a single bullet. He reared, pawing at the skies, just as he had in the white man's circus. Finally, while the great chief lay dying, the stallion bowed to him."

Tears pricked Sam's eyes.

"It's just a story," Jake said.

"I know it." Sam swallowed hard.

"A pretty widespread story," Kit insisted, "and ever after, the tribes said the white stallion honored his master with a final dance."

By the time they reached River Bend Ranch, they'd driven in silence for twenty minutes. Jake kept flashing Kit dirty looks, but Sam was sunk in melancholy over Norman White and her own stallion, not over Sitting Bull.

Still, she found the silence hard to break until she'd unloaded Ace. Even then, she thought her good-byes sounded mechanical.

"Nice meeting you, Kit. See you at school tomorrow, Jake."

"Tomorrow's Sunday," Jake reminded her, but Sam hardly heard.

More than usual, she felt the smooth gloss of leather reins, as she led Ace toward the barn. He hung back, tossing his head, tugging toward the ten-acre pasture.

Sam made a clucking noise to keep the gelding moving, and finally he walked after her. They'd crossed the ranch yard and passed the small pasture where Dark Sunshine and Tempest were spending their last day together before weaning, when Sam stopped.

She'd almost put Ace into the open box stall he'd shared with Sweetheart.

But Sweetheart was gone. The old paint mare lived in town. She served as a beloved therapy horse for disabled children and Gram went to work with her and the kids twice a week. Sweetheart had left three months ago, and Ace had been living in the ten-acre pasture even longer.

"What am I thinking, good boy?" Sam asked her bay gelding.

Ace didn't answer, just kept moving into the barn.

He stopped where she'd crosstied and groomed him dozens of times and waited for her to take off his tack.

Sam eased her saddle off and carried it to the tack room with Ace's bridle hooked over the saddle horn.

Much of Sam's tension drained away as she groomed her horse. She paid special care to avoiding Ace's ticklish spots—behind his elbows, under his belly, and especially his left flank—then cleaned his hooves and brushed him from poll to tail until not a single sweat mark remained.

Finally, Sam put all her grooming tools away, wrapped her arms around Ace's warm neck, and asked, "So what am I going to do, boy? Beg Dad to let me adopt the Phantom? That's not what either of us wants, but if that horrible Norman rounds him up, I can't let him go to someone else."

Ace nodded, and though Sam knew he was only rubbing his chin against her back, it felt like the bay gelding, who'd once roamed the Calico Mountains with the Phantom, was telling her it wasn't such a bad solution.

Then, something else broke.

She and Ace were leaving the barn when a gust of wind shook the structure, slamming the door in their faces, and the little wooden horse Dallas, River Bend's foreman, had carved and stained with white shoe polish to look like the Phantom flew off the ledge where Sam had poised it for good luck. It struck her head and fell on the floor.

The collision with her head should have slowed the figure enough to prevent damage, Sam thought as it landed on the hay at her feet. She wasn't worried as she bent to retrieve it, until she saw that one thin wooden leg was missing. It had snapped off. Though the leg wasn't hard to find, when she tried to fit the two pieces together, they didn't match. Sam searched for a wood chip and couldn't find one. Even if she glued the pieces back together, the white horse wouldn't be the same.

First Jake's windshield had cracked, then the coffeepot, and now this.

As she tucked the wooden pieces tenderly into her jacket pocket, Sam decided it was a good thing she didn't believe in omens, because bad ones were piling up all around her.

Sam was in the kitchen, setting the table and breathing in the tomato, onion, and cream aroma of Gram's swiss steak and scalloped potatoes, when she heard the BLM truck drive up.

"Brynna's a little . . ." Gram's voice trailed off and she moved from the kitchen counter to look out the window in the door. She wiped her hands on her apron and stared.

"What is it?" Sam asked, but she was already beside Gram.

They both watched as the BLM truck backed up, then rolled toward the bridge and back over the La Charla River. Brynna walked across the ranch yard, toward the house. Blaze bounced out to greet her, and Brynna ignored him.

That was totally unlike her, Sam thought. Brynna always had time to rumple the Border collie's ears. She hadn't crossed to the corral to greet her blind mustang Penny, either.

Sam heard the shower running upstairs. Dad was getting cleaned up for dinner. She wished he was here, now, because he was probably the only one Brynna would feel like talking to.

As she and Gram stepped back from the door, Sam noticed that Brynna lifted her chin and pinned back her shoulders before stepping up onto the porch.

"Last day of work," Brynna said. She tried to put a chirp in her tone, but her voice quavered and her blue eyes were filled with tears.

"I thought you had two more weeks," Gram said.

"So did I." Brynna stopped, pressing her shaking lips together for a second before she could go on. "But the D.C. office phoned to say they were going with my earlier leave date, that he . . ." She lifted a hand toward the truck and Norman White, though they were gone. "He . . . ," she repeated, but she couldn't finish.

When Gram tried to wrap her in a hug, Brynna stepped away. "Please don't. I can't fall apart, and if you —"

"I understand," Gram said, but she linked her

hands together as if it were the only way she could keep from comforting her daughter-in-law.

"He drove me home because I won't have access to a BLM vehicle until my leave ends. I think he didn't want me to have an excuse to drive up there and return it and get in his way." Brynna gave a bitter laugh. "Can you believe the home office didn't even wait until Monday? Someone phoned to say I should take some time off to enjoy myself. As if I could, with him . . ."

Brynna shook her head once more, and then rushed for the stairs.

Sam's heart sank as she looked after her stepmother.

With her braid bouncing between her shoulder blades, Brynna looked like a distraught teenager.

"Careful on the stairs," Gram whispered, and Sam wondered why she bothered, because Brynna couldn't possibly have heard.

Chapter Five

Dinner was a little late that Saturday night.

When Brynna came downstairs holding Dad's hand, her pink thermal shirt was stretched to its limits over gray sweatpants and her eyelids were red from crying, but her wet hair was fragrant with shampoo and she no longer trembled.

Forks clinked on plates. Teeth chewed. Throats swallowed. And every time Sam thought she could stand the silence no longer, Dad frowned at her.

What did he think she was going to say? Gosh, she didn't want Brynna unhappy any more than Dad did. Not only did she care for her stepmother, but Brynna had been the only one standing between the Phantom and capture since the day they'd met.

Finally, Brynna drew a shaky breath and said, "Norman's proposed a fifty percent reduction of wild horses on the range."

Sam closed her eyes.

"He thinks this winter will have a bad impact on the horses' habitat, especially in the Calico Range. That contradicts my research, which shows the horses going into winter strong enough to stand up against the weather and then benefiting from the high moisture content in this winter's storms, which will mean huge growth in rabbit brush, bitter brush, and all kinds of bunchgrass."

Brynna was a biologist, Sam thought. Her opinions were backed up with facts. So, why didn't Norman believe her?

"How will they decide who's right?" Gram asked.

"Coin toss," Dad muttered.

"I hope not," Brynna said, smiling at Dad's loyalty. "I'm home for a while, though, and rather than harassing my Washington contacts every day, I'm going to help you with weaning Tempest," Brynna said, nodding to Sam. "You with holiday baking," Brynna said to Gram, then turned to Wyatt. "And you with some of Pepper's chores, since we're letting him go home for two weeks."

Sam wanted to beg Brynna to help her make emergency plans for the Phantom, but she'd wait a little while. She wanted to save his whole herd, too, but that seemed impossible. Her only choice, if they brought him in, was to take money from her college fund to pay the stallion's adoption fees.

And I will *stand up to you over that,* Sam thought, looking at Dad.

Misinterpreting her glare, Dad sat back from the table and fixed her with steady eyes.

"About the weaning," he said. "I'm still planning on loading that buckskin up first thing tomorrow morning and taking her to Clara's pasture, where she's out of sight and sound of Tempest. She can run around with Teddy Bear, Jinx, and those two yearlings."

"I know," Sam said. She looked down at the food on her plate without appetite.

"Dallas is right about it being the kindest thing," Gram said. "If we put her in the ten-acre pasture where she and Tempest can see each other, there'll be no end to the neighing and crying. If we make the separation quick and final—by that I mean just for three weeks, of course—it's like ripping off a Band-Aid. It will only hurt for a minute."

Sam had heard Dallas's Band-Aid comparison more times than she could stand, but she just nodded.

Brynna gave a little sniff, the only sign of her earlier tears, before she said, "Tempest has been doing great with the creep feeder. We don't have to worry about her nutrition."

That part was true. Sam was happy that Dad had constructed the feeding pen with an entrance just big enough for Tempest to get in and eat, but too small for Dark Sunshine to follow. Day by day, the foal had become less dependent on her mother's milk, so she'd really only miss her company.

Loneliness would be bad enough, Sam thought, and suddenly she knew Tempest wouldn't be the only one missing Dark Sunshine.

"May I please be excused to go out and visit them?" Sam asked. "I promise to do the dishes when I get back."

"Go ahead," Dad said. Though he sounded gruff, Sam knew he understood.

"Take your time," Brynna told her. "Your Gram and I can handle things in here."

It was nearly dark outside.

Sam hunched her shoulders against the wind and jammed her hands into her coat pockets as she crossed the ranch yard. If all the predicted storms blew in, she wouldn't be going anywhere without a hat, gloves, and scarf, as well as her jacket.

As soon as Sam stepped into the barn, she felt sure those storms would come. Moisture in the air always brought out a Christmas tree smell from the pine boards. The smell reminded her of the rainy night she'd stayed with Dark Sunshine through her labor and delivery of her foal. And though it was probably silly, instead of turning on the barn lights, Sam went to the tack room and retrieved the lantern she'd used for gentle illumination on that night.

A golden glow swung around Sam as she returned to the stall. Dark Sunshine and Tempest both crowded close at her arrival, but Sam couldn't help noticing the different expressions in the horses' eyes.

Tempest's eyes glowed with excitement, because Sam brought food and fun into her life. When Sam didn't rush into the stall to give her a filly massage, Tempest rocked into a half rear and squealed excitedly.

"In a minute, baby," Sam said, "And you be careful. You're getting to be almost as big as your mama."

Dark Sunshine was just over thirteen hands tall, and her black-shaded legs were delicate as a doe's.

As Sam slipped inside the stall, the buckskin's wide-browed face nudged her shoulder, but then Sunny stepped back.

Beneath her black forelock, Sunny's eyes were watchful, always expecting the worst.

You've never been happy here, Sam thought, but she didn't say the words, because there had been moments after Tempest's birth when Sunny's longing neighs toward the mountains had stopped. And once, at the river, she'd had a chance to flee with the Phantom and she hadn't.

Sam stepped closer to Sunny and slid her hands over the mare in long, loving strokes.

It wasn't Sunny's fault that she was cautious. The first time Sam had seen her, the mare had been dehydrated and half-starved. Used by wild horse rustlers to lure other horses into a trap, she'd been left behind, blindfolded, time after time.

Sam had saved her—she guessed *stolen* was more accurate—but the mare had been beaten and traumatized. Fear had made her so vicious, no one could get close enough to remove her blindfold. When the red bandanna had finally fallen off, the mare's panic had made Jake guess the mare had been kept in a dark stall for most of her life.

Watching her whirl with flattened ears and flared nostrils, he'd said, "She's half scared you'll put her in the dark, and half scared you'll bring her into the light."

Sunny's spirit might have healed if a terrible barn fire hadn't struck River Bend Ranch. All the other horses had been freed to run from the flames, but Sunny had been forgotten in the round pen. By the time Sam remembered her, the mare's chest had been bloody from pounding against the log rails. Then the mare had stampeded after the other horses.

On another night, Sam's heart would have sung to see Sunny passing all the bigger horses—first Tank, then Sweetheart, Strawberry, Ace, and even long-legged Popcorn—but it hadn't been a beautiful sight. Terror had spurred the tiny mare to race for the lead.

"And it was so sad," Sam whispered, "when the Phantom brought you back."

Sad but amazing, too, Sam thought.

After guarding the buckskin jealously for weeks, the Phantom had returned her, driving her with snapping teeth back across the river to the ranch, where she'd get the human help she needed to heal her cuts.

Sunny had never stopped longing toward the Calico Mountains. So, a few weeks before, Sam had gone with Dad to check every post and crosspiece of the fence around Clara's pasture. The mare should be safe there. Even if she wanted to escape, her slim legs were too short to launch her over the rails to freedom.

"You might like being with Jinx and Teddy Bear," Sam told Sunny. Totally unaware of Sam's melancholy, Tempest nuzzled her neck with tickling whiskers. "And I'll stay with your silly girl."

Sam wrapped her arms around the little buckskin's neck, buried her face against her black mane, and breathed in its leather and straw sweetness. Though Dark Sunshine struggled against the hug, Sam gave her one more squeeze.

"Tempest will be safe with me," Sam promised, and then she let Sunny pull away.

On Monday afternoon, Sam thought she was probably seeing things.

It would make sense that she was having hallucinations. No one on River Bend Ranch had been able to sleep Sunday night, after Dark Sunshine had been taken away and Tempest had realized she was truly alone.

Sam had fought dozing off in class all day. She'd longed to, but it was a good thing she hadn't. Every teacher seemed determined to jam-pack the last few days of class before winter break with all the work that hadn't been accomplished the rest of the semester.

After school, Sam had trudged up the steps and onto the school bus, but the driver had turned up the heater as they'd driven along, and Sam had finally fallen asleep.

Slumped against the shoulder of her best friend Jennifer Kenworthy, Sam had only just started awake when the bus driver put on the loud air brake and jerked to a halt at Jen and Sam's stop.

"C'mon, sleepyhead," Jen had said, shrugging her shoulder under Sam's ear.

"Huh?" Sam had licked her lips and looked around the bus. Several people seemed to be staring at her. "Did I just yell? Is that why everyone's staring at me?"

"Yeah," Jen said, lifting Sam's backpack along with her own, "but I think it was the drooling that really caught their interest."

"You're awful," Sam muttered. She kept her eyes downcast as she followed right behind Jen, practically stepping on her heels.

"Me?" Jen said. "I wasn't the one snoring."

"Really?" Sam asked, horrified, as she hopped off the last step and watched the yellow bus depart.

"No, not really. Here, take this," Jen said. She helped Sam shrug into her backpack, then started walking. "And hey," she said, looking over her shoulder and motioning Sam to catch up, "just before you fell asleep, I asked you to go ride with me this afternoon and you made some excuse involving Kit Ely." Jen waggled her white-blond eyebrows suspiciously. "It got kind of garbled because you were babbling against my sweater."

Sam blinked, stared at the range spreading away from them, then hefted her backpack higher and hurried after Jen.

"Oh, yeah! Let's ride tomorrow. Because, since Kit is a Darton High graduate and he nearly made it to the National Finals Rodeo, Mr. Blair thinks I should interview him. I already called from Journalism class and I'm going to ride over there this afternoon."

Jen gave a breathy imitation of a wolf whistle, then added, "Cool! And are you taking pictures, too?"

"You have a boyfriend—"

"Just *looking*, Samantha—"

"—and though Kit Ely is cute—"

"Guys over twenty are handsome, attractive, or maybe even *fine*-looking, but not cute," Jen corrected.

"That's my point," Sam said, but a yawn erased most of her sarcasm. "Kit's twenty-five or twenty-seven, something like that, and he's way too old for you."

"Uh-huh, whatever, as long as he still has all of his teeth." Jen pretended to brush away Sam's advice.

Laughing, they'd nearly reached the spot where Jen cut left toward Gold Dust Ranch and Sam walked on to River Bend, when two things happened at once.

The powder-blue Mercedes driven by Mrs. Coley to take Rachel Slocum back and forth to school passed them and Rachel ducked out of sight. Next, a mechanical racket roared across the range.

Turning practically in a circle to find the source of the sound, Sam asked, "Am I hallucinating?"

"Doubtful," Jen said. Raising the frames of her glasses by their hinges and repositioning them, she gazed after the Mercedes. "I saw Rachel playing duck-duck-goose, plus I hear that noise. And, though I've read of mass hysteria with shared hallucinations, they occurred during the Middle Ages and were attributed to a mold peculiar to rye bread. Still, we *did* both eat in the cafeteria—"

"Shut up," Sam said, grabbing her friend's arm. "Look!"

A black helicopter bobbed up over the ridge to their right, bringing with it a hurricane of dust. Jen cupped her hands over her glasses. Sam held down her wind-crazed hair and tried to keep the blowing dirt out of her eyes, nose, and mouth.

The chopper was so low to the ground, Sam could see two men in the cockpit. The pilot wore mirrored sunglasses and the man beside him pointed excitedly, stabbing his index finger downward, straight at Jen and Sam.

Chapter Six

Sam had never studied the skilike things—skids, she thought they were called—that acted as helicopters' feet, but when this one banked away from her and Jen, and swung toward War Drum Flats, she got a closeup view. Too close.

Jen grabbed Sam in a hug.

"What—?" Sam began.

"I-i-if I can't hang on to someone, I'll be screaming like a k-kindergartner, so just humor me, okay?"

"Sure," Sam said. She'd rarely seen Jen frightened. Jen was so logical and levelheaded, Sam wondered if it was a mistake that she wasn't scared, too. A few seconds later, when Jen's trembling ended, Sam said, "Crazy, huh?"

Jen shook like a wet dog. Then she flipped her white-blond braids back over her shoulders and asked, "Do you know what that was?"

"A helicopter flying for BLM?"

"No," Jen said adamantly.

"I'm pretty sure it was," Sam said gently. "The guy sitting next to the pilot was Norman White."

Sam could practically see her friend's thoughts come together. Jen blinked owlishly, then said, "That may be, but the insignia on the helicopter says it's part of the predator and rodent control unit, and what scared me is—well, there are lots of rumors. . . ." Jen looked up and wrapped her arms around her ribs, as if she were trying to hide herself. "At least I *hope* they're rumors—about them spraying poison and using automatic weapons."

Sam felt a lurch of alarm, then told herself she shouldn't give in to her friend's fears. It was her turn to be the sensible one. She tried a joke.

"Regardless of how some senior boys act, we don't look like rodents," Sam teased. "Probably not predators, either. Besides, you're almost home."

"What about you?"

"I'll hustle toward River Bend, but from what I know about Norman White, I think I'll be safe. He's been a total jerk to Brynna and will be even worse to the wild horses, but he's also a by-the-book bureaucrat. He'd faint if he sprayed two innocent high school girls with—"

"Malathion?" Jen suggested.

"Right," Sam said, guessing Jen had named some kind of poison.

"Okay," Jen said, and Sam's common sense had erased the quaver in her voice.

Then, winter sun glaring on the helicopter's rotor blades made both girls squint after it.

"He's headed into Lost Canyon," Jen said.

First War Drum Flats and now Lost Canyon, Sam thought. Both areas had wild horse watering holes.

"He's coming up. Wait, no, he's dropping back down," Jen said, standing on her toes as the helicopter vanished. "Probably to check out Arroyo Azul."

Sam pictured the helicopter flying between the adobe-colored cliffs, following the turquoise stream twisting below. It was the first place she'd ridden the Phantom. The idea of the helicopter invading that place made her sick.

But wild horses were fast and elusive. She'd seen them outsmart humans many times, starting with the day she'd returned home from San Francisco.

She'd been riding with Dad in his old blue truck when a helicopter appeared, herding a band of wild horses. That day she'd felt herself running with the mustangs, feeling their fear, their determination to escape, and their excitement as they evaded capture.

That day, she hadn't known the names War Drum Flats, Lost Canyon, or Arroyo Azul. Now she did. Clearly she wasn't the only one. This helicopter wasn't flying random patterns.

"They're after mustangs," Sam said, feeling defeated.

"Not in that helicopter," Jen insisted.

"I hope you're right," Sam said.

Jen stopped at the path she'd follow to her house at Gold Dust Ranch. Before she said good-bye, Jen promised to call Sam if she discovered what was up with Rachel. In turn, Sam vowed to hurry home just in case the black helicopter really was spraying something toxic over the range.

True to her word, Sam took long steps and set her shoulders against the straps of her backpack as if she were a plow horse—not because she was afraid, but because she couldn't wait to talk to Brynna.

Sam scanned the winter range and shivered. Patches of snow showed in the shade of boulders. Clumps of sagebrush looked more gray than green. Though high desert plants were hardy, below-freezing temperatures tested them every night.

Winter was here. Sam missed the Phantom, but she hoped he was safely tucked away in his secret valley for the winter.

Glancing up, she saw that the ice-blue sky was empty. She didn't hear the helicopter, either.

Maybe Norman White had just been surveying the territory he was taking over, Sam thought. Or maybe the predator and rodent control guy was a friend, taking him for a ride.

Yeah, right, Sam thought.

Just two days ago, she'd heard Norman call the Phantom a *troublemaker*. Then he'd declared that the gray stallion should be taken off the range. As that conversation resurfaced in her mind, Sam stopped walking.

There was a flaw in her plan to use her college money to pay the Phantom's adoption fee.

Norman White had said the Phantom was feral, not wild, and he said BLM should hold the Forsters responsible for trespass fees that had been adding up over the years the stallion had roamed public lands.

Sam sucked in a breath of chilly air and resumed walking. There was no way Dad would let her take that much money from her college account. After all, she'd be graduating in two and a half years.

Whup-whup-whup.

The chopper had not gone home and landed. Sam heard it again.

The machine had managed to navigate the eastern canyons, and now it was circling back from the direction of Deerpath Ranch.

"No!" Sam shouted.

Two horses galloped below the helicopter. They crashed through the sagebrush side by side, veering around slippery snow spots, jumping thorny brush, and swerving around boulders.

A bay and a chestnut. Not from the Phantom's herd, but they looked familiar. Why did she recognize the horses?

The bachelors! When New Moon, the Phantom's midnight-black son had been evicted from his father's herd, he'd found companionship and safety with these two young stallions.

Yellow Tail and Spike, Mrs. Coley had called them, and though it had been a long time since Sam had seen Spike—a bay whose black mane stuck straight up—she'd seen Yellow Tail last fall.

Sam had a quick impression that Spike looked more filled out and male, but Yellow Tail had turned slim and graceful. His flaxen mane and tail rippled like silk. His coat was the color of gold in the heart of a flame.

Last year he'd looked pretty ragged from watching out for his two mares. He'd challenged the Phantom for a drinking place at the river and they'd fought. The battle had been confined to kicks until the stronger and more experienced Phantom had feinted a bite at Yellow Tail's foreleg and the golden stallion had tripped.

Sam couldn't imagine the chestnut confronting the Phantom now. Then the horses did something that intensified Sam's confusion.

With the helicopter right behind them, why were the young stallions slowing from a gallop to a lope? Why, with heads high and froth blowing from open mouths, were they slackening their pace even more, lifting their knees in a nervous trot?

Because the helicopter was herding them toward

the highway, Sam realized. The horses knew that danger screamed by on that asphalt river and they didn't dare cross it.

Or maybe, Sam thought as she noticed the horses' alert expressions, Yellow Tail and Spike had seen her and judged her as a nearer and more dangerous threat. Should she hide?

She was about to, when the two stallions displayed their strategy for escape. They turned sharply right, accelerated into a swift run, then skidded down the bank of the La Charla River.

A flock of wild geese burst up from the river. Disturbed by the stallions, the black-and-gray geese spread their wide wings and gave a few honks. Then they coasted on air currents above the water before climbing and banking away from the helicopter, making the manmade flyer look clumsy by comparison.

Running toward the river with her backpack slamming against her spine, Sam listened past her own panting. She didn't hear a splash or the clash of hooves on river rocks, not even the lash of willow branches on sweaty horsehide. She heard nothing but the hovering helicopter.

If the stallions headed upstream and veered west toward Aspen Creek, they could wend through white-barked trees and frosty black boulders. They'd be hard to pick out against that background, wouldn't they?

And if they traveled downstream . . .

Sam sawed her teeth against her lip, hoping they

wouldn't. There'd be little camouflage and they'd end up crossing the highway, after all, presenting themselves right into the sight of the men above.

But wait, Sam thought. She could guess where the horses were going because she knew this land. Norman White didn't. To him, the creeks and gullies were lines on a map.

The helicopter floated above the river for a few minutes, then lifted higher and hovered. At last, it soared higher yet, drifted southwest, then flew toward Willow Springs Wild Horse Center.

Sam sighed in relief. For now, the two young stallions were safe.

"Brynna!" Sam yelled as she collapsed into a kitchen chair. "Gram?"

Sam heard only the grandfather clock's pendulum. Then there was a thump, followed by soft footsteps. The swinging door between the living room and kitchen opened. Brynna, in stockinged feet but otherwise dressed just as she'd been last night at dinner, wandered into the kitchen, rubbing her eyes.

"I'm sorry," Sam apologized. "Were you napping?"

Brynna stared at Sam with a droopy smile. Then her eyelids fluttered closed.

"Oh no, you don't," Sam said. She pushed out of her chair so quickly, its legs squeaked on the kitchen floor.

Just last week, Brynna had actually fallen asleep standing up. Outside.

That time, Dad had caught her, but she and Brynna were almost the same size, and Sam wasn't sure she could.

"Try this," Sam offered, slipping a chair behind Brynna.

"I'm fine. Just sleepy," her stepmother insisted, but she sat. Her eyes were open and alert as she tightened the holder around her low ponytail and asked, "Was I dreaming or did I really hear a helicopter?"

"I wish you'd been dreaming, but you weren't," Sam said, and then she told Brynna what she'd seen.

Brynna shook her head vigorously. "I don't see how he could have received clearance for a gather yet. Not that it's my job anymore, but I'm calling my boss—my old boss," she amended, "in Reno to double-check."

"Good," Sam said.

"It's interesting that you saw Yellow Tail with his bachelor buddy," Brynna said.

"What do you think happened to his mares?" Sam asked.

Brynna gave an unconcerned shrug. "Few wild stallions under five years old actually win mares. They find them wandering and then a more mature stallion usually steals them. The Phantom is a rare exception."

"What about New Moon?" Sam asked. "The last

time I saw him he had two mares—a red bay and a bald-faced mare with a foal."

Sam didn't say she'd mentally named the foal Night the time she'd spotted the wild bunch up by Cowkiller Caldera.

"He might be like his daddy and hang on to them," Brynna said, but a shadow crossed her face.

Was Brynna thinking about Norman's plan to remove half the wild horses from the range?

"He wouldn't take New Moon *and* the Phantom, would he?" Sam felt dizzy with dismay, and it only got worse when Brynna didn't answer.

If the Phantom and New Moon were rounded up, they'd probably be gelded, to make them easier to handle and more likely to find adoptive homes.

If Night was brought in, too, and the herds of both stallions were dispersed to adopters all over the country—and that was the *best* she could hope for, Sam realized—the bloodlines of the legendary Phantom Stallion would hit a dead end.

It would be as if the silver mustang had never existed.

Chapter Seven

"Don't be surprised if it looks like the North Pole in there," Jake told Sam as she rode into the ranch yard at the Three Ponies Ranch an hour later.

"It's cold?" Sam guessed as she dismounted, casting a glance at smoke curling from the ranch house chimney.

"No, decorations. For Kit," Jake said. "I'll take Ace. You go on into Santa's workshop and do your *interview*."

"Okay," Sam said. She didn't trust Ace to many people, but Jake could take better care of her bay gelding than she could.

She started for the stone ranch house, then took a quick look back over her shoulder.

Jake had put a weird emphasis on that last word, but why? He'd sometimes implied he thought it was cool that she was on the *Darton Dialogue* staff. He'd even hinted that she'd done a good job on a locker vandalism story. So he wasn't putting her down.

It would be unlike him to be jealous, she thought, then corrected herself. Well, not *totally* unlike him. But the *Dialogue* had published a story about his cross-country running victories, so he and Kit would be even after she wrote up this interview.

"Hi, Samantha!" Mrs. Ely's cheeks were flushed, her blond hair flyaway, and she wore an apron over her teacherly slacks and shirt. "Come in and have some gingerbread. It's almost ready."

Sam hadn't noticed Mrs. Ely's Honda outside and she was surprised her history teacher was already home. Mrs. Ely was one of those teachers who arrived early and stayed late, giving makeup tests, tutoring, and grading papers.

And the house—wow, Jake had been right. There were candy canes hanging everywhere. An arrangement of pine boughs, gold bells, and red bows took up so much of the kitchen table, the cooling racks of gingerbread boys and girls barely fit, and Sam did a double take when she spotted Kit sitting amid it all.

He raised one hand in greeting as Mrs. Ely asked, "Need a refill on that cocoa, honey?"

"I'm good, Mom," he said, then, shrugging his shoulders inside what was clearly a brand-new plaid flannel shirt, added to Sam, "She's spoiling me. Wanted to put glitter on my cast."

He sounded so much like Jake, Sam had to smile.

"Well, it would have looked cute," Mrs. Ely said, but Sam could tell she was laughing at herself for fussing over her adult son.

Jake and Nate jostled for space in the doorway, bringing a blast of fresh air into the warm kitchen.

"Digger's decided he's a rodeo bronc," Nate said.

Sam pictured Nate's clean-limbed brown horse with the white chin spot as Nate pointed at Kit and added, "Must be your fault, bringing buckin' bugs home."

"Good horse like him, just brace your arms, keep his head up, and drive him forward," Kit suggested.

"Yeah," Nate agreed.

"Smells good, Mom," Jake said, but as he stripped off his leather gloves and held his hands near the open oven, he stared at Kit. Actually, more at Kit's arm, Sam thought.

"Help yourself," Mrs. Ely said. Then, as she piled cookies on a plate, she smiled at Sam and asked, "Why don't you two take your interview into the living room?"

"Fine," Kit said, standing.

As Sam took a small notebook and pen from her pocket, she noticed Jake reaching for a cookie. His mom whisked the plate out of reach and handed it to Kit.

Though every kitchen surface was covered with treats, Jake looked as if his mother had slammed a door in his face.

Kit must have noticed, because he jerked his head toward the living room and asked, "You comin', Baby Bear?"

Jake shook his head. Sam knew the lure of cookies and listening in on the interview wasn't enough to get Jake to answer to his childhood nickname.

She almost told Jake not to be such a baby. After all, he called her Brat all the time and she tolerated it, but when Sam tried to meet Jake's eyes, he turned away.

Sam followed Kit into the living room and jotted down a few setting details as background for her story.

She'd heard kitchens called "the heart of the house." At River Bend, that was true. Here at Three Ponies Ranch, though, she'd give that title to the living room.

The bushy pinion pine tree, probably cut nearby, boasted about a hundred fat, multicolored lights and almost as many ornaments, made by each of the six brothers in elementary school.

Sam noticed a pink felt pig with one blue sequin eye, a handprint covered in aluminum foil with "Quinn" scrawled across it in smudged black crayon, a clothespin angel missing half of her glued-on hair, and leather pony ornaments with cutout middles that framed photographs of each of the six boys on horses.

Turning her eyes from the Christmas tree, Sam saw an Indian print rug with geometric shapes in bright colors spread in front of the fireplace. Turquoise, amber, and purple bottles collected in the desert sat on glass shelves in every available window, casting multicolored beams as if the windows were made of stained glass.

A pine-planked wall displayed some of Mrs. Ely's photographs. Last year, she'd told Sam windows were her favorite things to photograph, and the pictures mingled with those of the Ely boys and their father, Luke. All black-haired and mahogany skinned, the Elys fished, barbecued, squatted awestruck next to a litter of barn kittens, and showed off every stunt humans could do on horseback.

"These make me wish I'd had brothers or sisters," Sam said, but when she turned to Kit, she saw he wasn't listening. He frowned as he flexed the fingers sticking out of his cast.

Quickly, Sam stared into the fireplace, listened to the others banging around in the kitchen, and waited for Kit to say something.

Because he was a male Ely, she knew that it could take a while. Sam pretended she was fascinated by the wreath hanging over the hearth.

But it turned out Kit had been listening.

"Guess you'll have one soon enough," Kit said. "A brother or sister."

"That's true," Sam managed as Kit gestured toward a scarred leather couch piled with pillows. "Thanks."

She sat, and Kit walked slowly to the chair nearest the blazing fire. At first Sam thought his lazy stride was another family trait, like Jake's tomcat-sleeping-in-the-sun squint, but then she wondered if Kit's legs hurt.

What did a bronc's first jump out of the chute do to the knees you held on with?

She hadn't meant to be so obvious, watching him, but he caught her.

"We don't need this on," Kit said. He advanced on the television, but only turned it down, not off.

Last year's Journalism class had taught Sam not to ask interview questions that could be answered with a yes or no, so she started out by taking Kit back to his Three Ponies childhood.

He remembered telling her that according to Shoshone legend, Jake had once been a horse and she'd been a mosquito.

"You guys were so little then," Kit said. "I had to hold Jake up so he could sneak cookies off the kitchen counter, or get his boot into a stirrup. And when he couldn't catch up with the rest of us, I let him ride on my shoulders."

This was so different from the dare he'd thrown down in the truck, about finding a couple of wild horses to see which of them was the real horseman of the family. Sam wished Jake had been sitting right beside her to see the wistful look on Kit's face.

Since she couldn't exactly call Jake in and make him look, Sam continued the interview by asking Kit about his vision quest.

He looked surprised that she'd heard about it.

"I was here when your grandfather insisted Jake do his—" Sam broke off, not sure how to go on.

"Indian initiation ceremony?" Kit joked.

Sam nodded. "Jake caught and tamed this amazing pinto mare, and then he let her go."

Kit gave a satisfied nod, but he didn't say anything, so Sam kept talking.

"Adam made a canoe, right? Nate was a fancy dancer, Quinn did drumming, and Bryan . . . I can't remember . . ."

"Built the sweat lodge. After I was gone, of course."

Kit called his vision quest a week of sleeping on the ground, fasting, and thinking about what he wanted to do with his life.

"Grandfather was so disappointed." Kit shrugged. "I'm surprised he made the rest of 'em do it."

"How could he have been disappointed?" Sam asked.

"He said I left home and never really came back," Kit said with a sigh. "But I just figured out that I was in love with rodeo. College wasn't for me—at least not then."

After that, Sam found it easy to get Kit talking about his life since leaving Three Ponies Ranch.

"Mostly it's boom or bust," he admitted. "On a night that the broncs are good to me, I sleep in a hotel room with as many of my buddies as we can squeeze in, but not before we play cards and eat our fill of room service steaks and salads."

"Salads?" Sam blurted.

"Yeah, most of us drive from rodeo to rodeo—the big guys fly, of course—but the way I did it, I had to eat too much fast food. It has to be something I can eat while I drive. So a big leafy thing that hasn't been fried can taste like heaven."

Taking notes, Sam noticed that Kit talked about his career as if it were over. She shook her head and scolded herself for being so literal.

"And the bust part?" she asked.

Kit chuckled. "Next night, it'll feel like the broncs have been talking, deciding they let me off too easy, and since I spent all my winnings the night before, I'll end up sleepin' on a blanket in some fairgrounds barn."

"That must be hard," Sam said.

"It pays off, mostly. I mean, I almost made it to the Grand Nationals."

So it had been true, Sam thought. She jotted a note—not that she'd need reminding later—that the boy from Three Ponies Ranch had made it to the top.

When Sam looked up, though, Kit was rubbing

the fingers on his casted arm. He met her eyes and gave a self-mocking smile.

"If I hadn't gone to that one last rodeo, training for the big time, I wouldn't have wrecked my arm or had to take out a loan on my truck to pay doctor bills."

"I don't know much about it, but isn't there, like, medical insurance for you?" Sam asked.

"For the big guys," Kit said again. "And the Justin Boot company has a cowboy crisis fund, but when you see what happens to some riders, this"—he lifted his cast—"is nothing. I'd be ashamed to apply."

Kit looked down as his mother came into the living room followed by Jake and Nate. After leaving home and staying gone so much, was Kit ashamed to ask for help with his medical expenses? Had he arrived on foot because he'd had to sell his truck? Sam wondered.

"Kit, Sam, will it bother you if we sit in on your interview?"

"We're almost done, anyway," Sam said. She glanced at the television and saw the evening news coming on. If she didn't hurry she'd be riding home in the dark. "I only have one more question, and it's kind of sappy."

"Fire away," Kit told her.

"All the kids at Darton High, your old school, will be wondering how it feels to live your dream. What would you tell them?"

Sam expected Kit to shrug, as Jake might have. Instead, Kit stared into the fireplace, then sat back in his chair.

When Kit spoke again, his voice had taken on the storytelling tone he'd used for the tale of Sitting Bull and the dancing white stallion.

"Well, Samantha, I've been pretty fortunate. That's all. I've drawn lots of mostly good horses and most times I've stuck on 'til the buzzer. I managed to duck injuries, trucks that broke down in the rain, and bad luck. . . .

"After this heals," Kit continued, lifting his cast, "I see myself back at the chutes, helping Pani—he's my best buddy, a cowboy from Hawaii, if you can believe it—tie on his riggin', havin' him give me a high five, even after I beat him out in the arena."

"Is that really how it is?" Nate asked. "Your friends don't get mad if you beat them?"

"Most don't," Kit said. "I've seen a man loan his ten-thousand-dollar horse as easily as you'd loan Sam here a pencil in school. And if a pal gets injured, we have fund-raisers and kick in whatever we can to help him."

"But it's such a vagabond lifestyle, going from place to place without a family," Mrs. Ely fretted.

"When you're that far from home, you kinda make your own neighborhood," Kit told his mother. "Then you haul it around with you from state to state, rodeo to rodeo, like a snail with its shell."

Kit swallowed so hard that Sam heard him, before going on, "Mom, I love rodeo. It's just flat-out different from other sports. Cowboys don't boo when the judge makes a call they don't like. Oh, there might be boots scuffin', or men pullin' their hats down a little harder than's called for, but that's all. The fans don't go out and trash the town for a celebration, either. That sort of behavior just ain't our style.

"Basically—and Sam, you know this from my brothers and your own dad—cowboys don't tolerate no whining." Kit was quiet for a few seconds as he stared at his cast. "You just gotta take it as it comes."

Chapter Eight

Sap sizzled inside a log in the fireplace, then popped. Sam breathed in the smells of gingerbread, wood smoke, and damp flannel shirts.

"I'm proud of you," Mrs. Ely said simply.

Nate groaned and held his throat as if his mother's sentimentality made him sick. Then Quinn clomped in from the kitchen, hollering to ask where everyone was, and Sam snapped her notebook closed. The interview was over. It was time she let the Elys get back to being a family.

"I've got what I need. Thanks, Kit," she said. Feeling like a professional journalist, she leaned down to shake his good hand, and told him, "Don't get up."

Then she glanced at Jake to see if he planned to walk outside with her to get Ace.

From the corner of her eye, Sam had kept track of Jake's reaction to his brother's remarks.

He'd shifted, cleared his throat, and thrown his arm over the back of his chair. Even if he'd been bored, she'd expected to see Jake smiling now.

That wasn't what she saw.

Jake's reaction reminded her of a snowstorm. When you glimpse the first few snowflakes, you're not even sure they're there. You blink, thinking you're seeing things, guessing it's just blowing off trees or rooftops, but then, suddenly, flurries turn into fury.

Jake looked angry. He must feel jealous of Kit's lifestyle, independence, and success. He was probably too embarrassed to admit it, but resentment had been bubbling up in him since Kit arrived home. She didn't want to be nearby when it boiled over.

I'm out of here, she thought, giving a quick wave, then heading out of the living room. She heard Jake's boots and the chime of his spurs following her through the kitchen.

He's just going to be surly, Sam warned herself when she was tempted to stop.

So she walked faster. She'd made it outside to the front porch when she noticed the deepening dusk. She had to hurry home.

"I forgot how much I hate it when he plays people."

Jake's voice made her glance back.

"What?"

"I keep trying to remember the good times, but when he does that thing—"

"What thing?" Sam asked.

"Reeling folks in, like he did just now." Jake jerked his head toward the house. "Like he did tellin' you about Sitting Bull."

That wasn't playing people, Sam thought; *it was weaving words into great stories.* It might even be charm, but she didn't tell him that.

"You can do the same thing," she said, seeing the skill in a flash of memory. "When you told me about the three Indian ponies your ranch is named for and the star shower—"

"I don't use that sad smile to make people go gooey-eyed."

Just leave, Sam told herself, and she stepped off the porch.

"You guys will work it out," she said airily, but Kit's wistful expression as he recalled boosting little Jake up to reach things crowded out her good intentions. "Jake, that's a real smile."

Just as he'd welcomed Witch's misbehavior, he welcomed Sam's.

"And you'd know that, better 'n me," Jake scoffed, "after spendin' *how* much time with him?"

Jake was rarely sarcastic, so she tried to stay calm. But when he leaned against the house with his arms crossed and gave a scornful sniff, that did it.

"I *know,*" Sam snapped as she marched closer to Jake, "because I was paying attention when he was talking about *you* before you and Nate came into the room—"

"Don't point your finger at me, Samantha."

"Okay," she said, then poked her index finger against his chest.

Jake sidestepped and left her hand hanging there until she dropped it to her side.

Then she tried being sympathetic. "Jake, I know it must make you crazy when Kit calls you Baby Bear—"

"Hold your voice down."

Sam took a deep breath. His request made her even madder. Did he think she wanted his family as an audience to this ridiculous discussion?

"What," she whispered, "did he have to gain by saying nice things about you when you weren't there to hear? Huh?"

"This," Jake said, and now he was the one pointing. "You standing up for him."

"I am so sure—" Sam broke off and stared into the lavender sky. Spotting the evening star, she made a hurried wish that she could smooth things over. "Jake, a twentysomething-year-old man doesn't care if a high school sophomore takes his side against his brother!"

Jake was in over his head. He didn't like to *talk,*

let alone dissect relationships.

So Sam gave him a minute. She heard Ace nicker. She made out the garbled noise of the television inside the Elys' house. She saw Jake scuff his boot toe in the dirt as he muttered, "I don't know."

Sam looked down to snap her coat closed just as the front porch light suddenly glared down on them.

The kitchen door swung open, nearly striking Jake.

"Sam, don't go," Mrs. Ely said. "I'm not a gossip. Well, not usually," she corrected with a sheepish grin, "but honey, believe me, you've got to see this! You, too, Jake. I wish Luke were home," she fretted, glancing toward the ranch gates.

Then she turned to go back into the house.

Sam only stared at Jake for a second. Was he going to say something to erase his hostility?

"What?" she encouraged him, and then Sam waited.

She didn't want to be impatient, but her curiosity was stronger than her desire to continue their stupid conversation. So, when Jake mumbled "Nothin'" and stepped aside to let her squeeze past him, Sam slipped back into the house.

"That son of a gun had it coming!"

Sam followed Nate's crowing voice back into the living room.

Everyone was staring at the TV, but it took Sam

a few seconds to make sense of what the reporter's voice was saying. She recognized Lynn Cooper's throaty tone at the same time that she recognized two of the three men on the TV screen.

Linc Slocum, dressed in a brick-colored Western suit with embroidery on the lapels, stood outside the sheriff's office in Darton. He stood next to a businesslike man she didn't recognize, but nearby she was pretty sure, yeah, that was Sheriff Ballard.

Linc's slicked-back hair glinted and he flashed his toothpaste commercial smile at the camera before taking a dramatic drag on a cigarette and blowing a plume of smoke into the air.

"He is so—" Quinn began.

"Quiet! Listen!" Nate shouted.

". . . moments later, Lincoln Slocum was arrested for income tax evasion by federal agents of the Internal Revenue—"

"That's Linc!" Sam gasped.

"Good, Samantha." Quinn chuckled, patting her arm.

"Getting arrested!" Sam said, and then her jaw dropped as two other men in suits ignored the camera to briskly handcuff Linc. "Oh my gosh!"

She felt hot and cold at the same time. She couldn't believe her eyes. She should call Jen! She should call home!

"Take a deep breath, Samantha," Mrs. Ely said.

She did, then let it out with such a rush that even

Jake smiled a little.

Sam was still staring at the TV screen when a different face filled it. This reporter was interviewing a mechanic who was giving cold-weather tips for starting your car's engine in the morning. Why was she looking at this?

"So, why did they arrest him?" Sam sputtered, turning to face Mrs. Ely. "I heard it, but nothing sank in"—she swallowed, then continued in a wondering tone—"except Linc Slocum is going to jail."

"Income tax evasion," Mrs. Ely said. "That means he didn't pay taxes on some money he earned. He cheated the government and they came after him."

Sam's eyes wandered back to the TV screen, but she didn't see the dancing toilet brush in the commercial. As if she were watching a movie, she saw the scar on the Phantom's neck—inflicted by Linc. She saw the black eye of a rifle barrel, aimed at her by Flick—the criminal hired by Linc. She saw buffalo bulls charging through the Superbowl of Horsemanship, endangering Jen, because of Linc. She saw a dead cougar sagging in Linc's arms, and a dead mother coyote staring with sightless eyes.

She remembered standing right here in the Elys' living room watching coverage of Karla Starr's rodeo. She'd thought her heart had broken as she'd watched her beautiful Phantom in a wild horse race, bucking off a rider, only to have the stupid boy—Ben Miller, she even remembered his name!—grab the stallion's tail and hang on. Who could blame the Phantom for biting the boy's shoulder and shaking him like he was a rude colt?

But they'd called the silver stallion a man-eater.

He'd been muzzled in metal by the time Sam found him and she'd discovered her heart really hadn't broken before, because when the drugged stallion had staggered and fallen to his knees in front of her, *then* her heart had broken. All because Karla Starr had help catching the Phantom—help from Linc Slocum.

"After everything he's done," Sam heard her own high-pitched voice rising in disbelief, "they arrested him for not paying his taxes?"

"I swear, girl, you'd complain if they hung you with a new rope," Kit joked.

Sam sighed. Kit had been gone. He couldn't know all the awful things Linc had done.

"I guess you're right," Sam said. "It doesn't matter why, as long as they lock him up."

"Havin' a taste for vengeance is a nice quality in a girl, don't ya think?" Quinn asked, looking from Sam to Nate.

Mrs. Ely ignored her sons. "Actually, Sam, this might be better. When it comes to missing money, the feds make their charges stick."

"'The feds.'" Nate chuckled. "No more TV for Mom."

All at once, Sam wanted to dance in celebration.

Linc Slocum would get what was coming to him. But she didn't dance. She watched Bryan mime Slocum's arrest, then ducked the couch pillow Adam threw at him.

Before she could get caught in a family free-for-all, Sam headed for the door.

Chapter Nine

"Now I know I don't need to tell you this, but I'd be a bad grandmother if I didn't," Gram began the next morning as she drove Sam to the bus stop.

"Is this going to be a warning not to act happy because Linc Slocum's going to jail?" Sam asked.

"No gloating, is all," Gram said. "And bear in mind he's only been arrested—"

"And charged," Sam sang. After watching two newscasts last night, she knew what she was talking about.

Gram shook her head, laughing quietly. "You look very nice, by the way."

Sam considered her powder-blue sweater, best jeans, and brushed suede boots. The tip of her tongue licked out to taste her vanilla-flavored lip gloss and she shook the hair she'd conditioned and curled because she'd woken so early.

She wasn't gloating, but she might be celebrating just a teeny bit, Sam thought. And wasn't she entitled to do that? After two years of watching Linc Slocum get away with all kinds of what Gram herself had called "wickedness" last night, it was exciting to see justice come crashing down on him.

"I didn't mean to dress up for the occasion," Sam told Gram. "It just happened."

"Um-hmm," Gram said as she pulled up to the bus stop. "My goodness, I wonder what—" Gram stopped the Buick and rolled down its window. "Lila," she called out, "whatever are you doing here?"

Sam was surprised to see Jen's mother at the bus stop, too. She didn't remember ever seeing her here before. A glance back at Gram made Sam downright suspicious. Gram's openmouthed expression was half startled, half delighted, as if she thought something wonderful was about to happen.

And for the first time that she could remember, when Sam looked at Jen's mother, Lila's short blond hair looked springy, her face glowed, and Sam could absolutely see the cowgirl who'd won the Best in the West rodeo queen title.

What was going on? Last night she'd called Jen's house over and over again and no one had picked up the phone. Sam had decided, between calls, that

Mrs. Coley must have known about Linc's arrest yesterday, and that was why Rachel had ducked down in the backseat.

The Kenworthys had no answering machine, and Dad had made Sam quit dialing at nine o'clock. He didn't seem to care how eager she was to talk to Jen. When Sam had given in and gone to bed, she'd been too excited to even read.

She'd been wide awake when she heard Dad and Brynna climb the stairs, then come down the hall, talking quietly as they passed her open bedroom door.

"I'm sure they have a lot going on over there," Brynna had said.

"Worst-case scenario, Slocum sells the ranch to pay his back taxes," Dad had replied gloomily. "Then what do they do?"

Sam had fallen asleep worrying, imagining the Kenworthys moving into the ranch house at River Bend and Jen sharing her room, but now, she knew nothing bad had befallen the family.

Not when she saw how Jen was dressed.

Sam jammed the car door open and jumped out before Jen's mom even had a chance to answer Gram.

"You are too much!" Sam giggled as she took in Jen's green stretch pants, red sweater, and elf hat with a bell on its tasseled end.

"Like it?" Jen asked, her voice muffled behind

the hands she had pressed over her lips.

"Yeah."

Then Jen actually started bouncing up and down on her toes. The bell lashed around, tinkling, while Jen rolled pleading eyes toward her mother.

"Endorphins," Jen explained. "They're a chemical reaction to elation, euphoria, and exultation."

Lila ignored her daughter to talk to Gram.

"Hi, Grace," Lila greeted Gram. "I'm just here to make sure Jen gets on the bus all right."

"Mom, please don't fib," Jen begged, then whispered to Sam, "She's actually here to keep me quiet."

"Nothing's final yet, Jennifer. I'm sorry." Lila's faint Texas accent sweetened her words. "You'll have to wait with the rest of us until it is."

"But just Sam," Jen begged.

"You can tell Sam first, but that won't be until after school today. And only if it's smooth sailing. Get ready for it to be tomorrow or the next day if there are complications. And you *will* wait, young lady," Lila ordered.

Jen moaned. "If that happens, you'll be picking up shreds of your daughter spread all over the place, because I will have exploded from waiting!"

"That's disgusting, but I believe I can live with the possibility," Lila drawled, then returned to her conversation with Gram.

"Something good?" Sam whispered, shooting a watchful look after Lila.

"You don't even *know*!" Jen said, hugging herself.

Just then, gravel crunched on the road from Gold Dust Ranch and the Slocums' blue Mercedes rolled toward them. Mrs. Coley gave a quick wave to them all, but Rachel turned so that only the sleek curve of her coffee-colored hair showed.

"Mom," Jen said as the Mercedes turned right on the highway. "If Sam and I held hands and swung around in a circle, would it seem"—Jen stared skyward while thrumming her fingers against her chest—"I don't know . . . *insensitive*?"

Lila's jaw dropped, but Sam answered.

"That would be *gloating*," Sam scolded with mock seriousness. She barely got the words out before Lila and Gram reprimanded them.

"Jennifer!"

"Samantha Anne Forster!"

"Here comes the bus!" Jen shouted.

"You remember what I said," Lila called after Jen as the girls climbed onto the school bus.

"Yes, Mother," Jen agreed, mimicking her mother's drawl.

After that, Sam thought for sure Jen would confide the big secret as soon as she got on the bus. But she didn't.

Darton High School buzzed with rumors.

Linc Slocum, father of a Darton High student body officer and the most popular girl on campus, had been arrested. No one knew more than that, but the gossip kept flowing anyway.

To her surprise, Sam wasn't tempted to join in. She'd glimpsed Rachel between classes and almost felt sorry for her. The first thought that popped into Sam's mind was: *feeding frenzy.*

Crowds of students standing in front of their lockers shrunk out of Rachel's way. Then, as soon as she passed, the groups fused back together to chatter, point, and roll their eyes.

At lunch, Sam was standing with Jen when Rachel walked out of the main office carrying a sheaf of papers. Chin high, Rachel clicked past wearing a slim-fitting black dress, stiletto heels, and dark glasses.

"Even though this must be the worst day of her life, she manages to look great," Jen said, "like a totally fashionable widow."

Sam and Jen turned to stare at a group of letter-jacketed jocks guffawing loudly. They were just asking for people to notice them as they leered after Rachel.

"Those guys," Sam said, "would have kissed her shoes if she'd just smiled at them yesterday."

"And check this out," Jen said. She nodded toward a blond girl waving her hands to accompany her prattle as she stood surrounded by girls in Darton High spirit uniforms. "Daisy's totally deserted her."

"I don't exactly pity Rachel," Sam said slowly.

"But it's kind of unfair that she's getting treated this way because of something her dad did."

Jen nodded sympathetically, but the smile that hadn't left her face all day was still there.

Sam had walked into Journalism class and plopped her completed interview with Kit Ely into the hand-in basket in the back of the room before she spotted Rachel standing next to Mr. Blair. The rich girl—or maybe not, Sam thought abruptly—leaned one palm on his desk. Her manicured fingernails glittered as she talked to him and the angle of her head seemed to include Rjay, the newspaper editor who stood nearby, in the conversation, too.

"It's not a story for us," Mr. Blair's voice boomed.

He scrawled his signature on two sheets, then returned them to Rachel and for a second, Sam thought he was about to tell her to take off her dark glasses inside, but Mr. Blair ignored them. His tone was uncharacteristically gentle as he said, "Rachel, we're handing out December's issue tomorrow. Then there's the two-week winter break. You might want to think this through a little longer. This trouble could all blow over by January."

Sam couldn't hear Rachel's response as she took the papers, creased them in half, and slid them into her purse.

The bell rang, and for the first time all year, no one was tardy. By the way they all stared at Rachel,

Sam knew why.

Every student settled into a desk. Everyone, even crazy Zeke, watched silently as Mr. Blair made a be-my-guest gesture to Rachel. She wasted no time taking command of the classroom.

"Not that I owe any one of you an explanation—I'm doing this for myself," Rachel began. She started to cross her arms, then left them loosely at her sides. "I'm sure you're all aware that my father has encountered some legal trouble. Though Mr. Blair assures me this isn't a story for the *Dialogue,* I have a few things to say, just in case it becomes one and I'm not here to set things straight." Rachel started to put her hands on her hips, then once more forced her hands to stay palm in, at her sides.

She stared over everyone's heads at the center of the bulletin board on the back wall, even though Daisy seemed to be craning her neck to catch Rachel's glance.

"I'm returning to school in England. Tonight. My brother Ryan, for reasons that are completely beyond me, wants to take over the ranch, so he will. My father has very complicated financial affairs and has had for years. This is just a misunderstanding. He has the best tax attorney money can buy—"

Sam blinked in surprise as Rachel's lips lifted at one corner. Was that a smirk? Was she mocking her father? Herself? Her whole life based on money?

"—and we shall hope that is enough."

Rachel's head dipped in a little bow, like it had when she'd sung at the talent show at the beginning of the school year. Then, holding her black clutch purse in one fist, she stalked out of the room.

They listened as Rachel's high heels echoed down the corridor. They heard the door at the end of the hall open, then sigh closed.

Rjay scratched his head as he looked at his spellbound staff. "Anyone—"

And then the high heels were clicking back, coming closer.

Was she the only one holding her breath, Sam wondered, as the clicking stopped at the classroom door?

Even Mr. Blair looked astonished when Rachel held on to the door frame and leaned inside.

"There's only one of you I want to wish good-bye and good luck," Rachel said.

Daisy half rose from her seat, holding her hand against her chest, pretending to blink back tears.

Rachel jerked off her dark glasses and used them to point at Sam.

"You, cowgirl," she said in a mocking tone. "Of all the people at this school, you were the only one who was never a phony. You were never cool, and heaven knows you have the fashion sense of a—*Nevadan*—but there's not a fake bone in your body, either. Maybe, somewhere, that counts for something." Rachel slid her dark glasses back on without disturbing her glossy hair, then tilted her head to one side. "Help my brother with that stinking ranch, if you can, hmm?"

And then she was gone, and this time, when the door at the end of the corridor closed, it stayed that way.

"Does anyone else feel like they should applaud?" Rjay asked.

Amid a rustle of questions and voices, Zeke insisted on giving Sam a high five.

"Stop it," she said, face blazing with embarrassment.

"Fine, then. That's over. Everyone in this room owes me story ideas for the first issue after vacation," Rjay shouted. "And hey, you, 'Cowgirl' . . ." Rjay definitely *was* smirking, but with the good humor Sam expected from him. "How about you wipe the manure off your boots, grab your camera, and get on out to the quad?

"Next issue's our winter formal edition, and I can see through the window that it just started snowing. Get me a hazy, romantic shot for the front page—a couple who've sneaked away from their teachers to smooch would be nice—and I'll see that you pass this class."

Sam grabbed her camera, stuck out her tongue at her editor—a gesture Mr. Blair turned his head to miss—then went outside.

Soft snowflakes melted as they touched Sam's

cheeks. She was alone and she hoped the storm was just blowing through. She'd promised to ride with Jen this afternoon so that her friend could reveal what was going on.

It might only be the news Rachel had announced, that Ryan was taking over the Gold Dust Ranch, but maybe there was more. The way this day was shaping up, Jen's secret could be almost anything.

The weak storm had passed by the time Sam met Jen after school. As they walked toward the school bus, tromping footprints in the snow, Sam saw Jake striding toward his truck. After mulling over Jake's outburst, she'd decided to go with her first thought—Jake was just jealous of Kit. It would blow over.

So she decided to be the bigger person and take action to erase yesterday's squabble.

"What are you doing?" Jen asked as Sam dug her bare hands into the snow and yelped at the cold. "Tell me you're not going to put it down my neck." Jen pulled up the collar of her red sweater until it almost reached her ears.

"No, I'm"—Sam broke off, shaking the fingers of one hand to get feeling into them—"trying to make a snowball, but this snow is too soft."

Jen followed Sam's gaze across the student-packed parking lot, then glanced at the bus.

"Well you better just whitewash his face and hurry back. Mr. Pinkerton's been cranky lately." Jen nodded toward their bus driver, pacing next to their bus. "He won't wait for you."

"This won't take long," Sam promised.

She wasn't going to whitewash Jake's face. The snowball was falling apart even as she looked both ways, dodged a car backing up, and went after him.

Jake's hair was finally long enough again to be pulled back with a leather thong. It hid the collar of his denim jacket, and she aimed the snowball just below the straight line of his black Shoshone hair.

He dropped the books he'd been carrying and turned smiling, braced to scoop up a snowball of his own, until he saw her. Then, Jake's face blanked out. Just like that, it was expressionless.

"Hey, all I want's a friendly little snowball fight," she yelled.

She marched closer to him, holding her arms wide, making herself a perfect target, but Jake just bent, picked up his books, and brushed the snow off the bottom one.

"Your friend ain't here no more," Jake said.

Then he climbed into his truck, slammed the door, and carefully drove away.

Chapter Ten

"What happened?" Jen demanded, taking her backpack off the seat she'd saved for Sam and tugging her down to sit beside her. "If you'll pardon me," Jen hissed, "you look totally devastated."

"I'm not devastated," Sam said, though she felt as if she'd been punched in the stomach. "Jake's just being a jerk."

"What's wrong with him?" Jen asked.

Your friend ain't here no more. His words echoed in her head. Why would he say that?

"Who knows? It doesn't matter. What *does* matter is that yesterday, right after I left you, that black helicopter came back and it was herding two amazing stallions."

"Why would it go after two stallions—bachelors, I'm guessing, right?—when, for the same cost per helicopter hour, they could bring in a herd?"

"Jen," Sam said, about to accuse her friend of being heartless.

"I'm not saying that's what they should do," Jen pointed out. "I'm just looking at it as a mathematician."

"Or a BLM bureaucrat," Sam agreed, "like Norman White."

If he was going to reduce the horses on the range by half, that would mean gathering whole herds. *But please not the Phantom's,* Sam thought, *or New Moon's.*

"Are we still going riding?" Sam asked suddenly. She'd love another look at Yellow Tail. Something about the young stallion intrigued her.

Jen gave a little bounce in her seat.

"Yep, and if everything goes right," Jen said, brandishing two hands worth of crossed fingers, "will I ever have news for you!"

Melting snow dripped off the barn when Sam went out to hug Tempest before she grabbed her tack.

Dallas stood just inside, staring up at the roof, checking for leaks.

"Filly seems to be doing fine," Dallas said. Then, without lowering his gaze from the barn roof, he added, "Better than you, by that frown you're wearing."

"I'm okay," Sam said.

Dallas gave a nod.

"Your Gram gave me that wooden horse that got broke and I'm fixin' it."

Sam blinked. She didn't even remember where she'd put the carved horse, and yet Gram was looking out for her by asking Dallas to repair it.

"Thanks," she said. "It just fell in the wind, and . . ."

Dallas touched the brim of his hat. Then, with typical cowboy tolerance, he left her alone with her filly, understanding she didn't want to talk.

And she really didn't. Not about feeling sorry for Tempest because she'd been separated from Dark Sunshine. Not about Brynna, who was inside the ranch house driving Gram crazy by insisting she was going to clean the entire attic instead of just helping Gram bring down the Christmas decorations. Not about Spike and Yellow Tail and evil black helicopters. And certainly not about Jake.

Sam slipped inside Tempest's stall and wrapped her in a hug.

"I love you, baby," she said, nuzzling the filly's cottony mane. She sighed and the tension of the day eased away a bit.

The filly put up with Sam's human affection until she noticed her gloves.

With a snort, Tempest butted her black muzzle against Sam's hands.

"You've never seen me wear gloves before?" Sam asked.

Laughing, Sam backed up, gently batting at the

filly as she tried to nip the gloves off. Tempest was persistent, pursuing Sam around the stall, until both the filly and Sam were startled by the blasting of a horn.

"Samantha!" Dad shouted.

"What now?" Sam whispered at the filly. "Can I just hide in here?"

Taking advantage of Sam's distraction, Tempest caught the tip of one gloved finger and tugged.

"You little imp!" Sam said as the glove slipped free of her hand.

Tempest held her head high, flapping the glove as she lifted her knees in a proud prance.

Sam chased the filly, caught her around the neck, and pried the glove from her teeth.

"Yuck, horse spit," Sam joked, but Tempest probably couldn't hear the insult over the single prolonged blare from outside.

Sam knew she'd kept Dad waiting too long.

"Later for you, cutie," Sam said, kissing Tempest's face. The black filly pulled away and made one more openmouthed feint, but Sam escaped, happy and smiling as she wiggled her fingers back into her glove.

Dad's new gray truck sat right outside the barn.

"Hi!" Sam greeted him.

Dad reached across the cab and shoved open the passenger's side door. "Get in."

"I can't," Sam said. "Where are you going?"

"*We're* going to Darton."

"I can't," Sam repeated. "I'm meeting Jen for a ride."

And she's going to tell me a gigantic secret, Sam thought, but she kept that to herself. Dad would be far more sympathetic to a broken promise than chitchat.

"Nope, you're going to the Department of Motor Vehicles to test for a hardship driver's license."

"What? A driver's license? I only . . ." Sam gestured through the ranch gates toward the range.

A couple of weeks ago she'd driven this truck about six miles with Jake and Singer in the back. She hadn't known what she was doing. Jake had given her rudimentary instructions, but she'd killed the engine a bunch of times and been too afraid to drive it over the bridge.

Sure, they'd all arrived home safely. And yeah, Dad had practiced driving with her twice since then and it had turned out she was a natural at shifting from one gear to another, but the engine almost always died after she came to a stop. She'd thought the lessons were just for fun.

"Get in," Dad insisted. "We'll talk about it on the way." He tilted his head to look out the window at the sky, instead of looking at the clock on the truck's dashboard. "Not much daylight left and they close at five."

Sam's shoulders drooped. The grin Tempest had

put on her face sagged, too, but she could tell there was no sense trying to talk Dad out of this. His mind was made up.

"Can I at least call Jen and let her know?" Sam asked after she'd climbed into the truck and fastened her seat belt.

"Your Gram's taking care of that," Dad said, and they were off.

Although Sam was aching to hear Jen's news, she comforted herself with the possibility that maybe whatever it was hadn't become "final" yet, as Lila had cautioned Jen to expect.

A hardship driver's license. Sam turned the words over in her mind. Hadn't Jake had one of those? She couldn't remember, but she felt scared, rather than eager to get one.

"Kind of sudden, I know," Dad said, glancing over at her. "But I just thought, if you were alone with Brynna when she went into labor with the new baby . . ." Dad's voice trailed off.

"I'd be able to drive her to the hospital," Sam finished.

"Legally," Dad added. "You can read that."

Dad pointed to a handbook on the seat between them and Sam flipped through it. Though she shivered at the prospect of all the highway miles between home and town, and the likelihood of oncoming traffic, stop lights, and cars zooming up behind her and then passing in the other lane, she nodded.

Anything was better than being helpless, and she had to admit a swell of pride was almost choking her. When she'd come home to River Bend two years ago, she never could have guessed Dad would trust her with such a huge responsibility.

They'd driven for about ten minutes when Sam said, "Rachel Slocum's going back to England and she said Ryan's going to be running the ranch."

"Huh," Dad responded.

"Do you think he's cut out for it?" Sam asked.

"Not for me to say."

Of course not, Sam thought, feeling defeated.

After another mile, though, Dad added, "Jed thinks he could make a go of it."

Wow, was that the closest Dad had ever come to gossiping? Sam grinned.

"Did you talk to him about it?" Sam prodded for details.

"I saw his truck at Clara's when I checked on the buckskin."

"Sunny was okay, wasn't she?" Sam asked.

"Seemed to be," Dad said. "Jed was in havin' coffee."

Sam pictured Jed Kenworthy, foreman of Gold Dust Ranch, at Clara's on the day after Linc's arrest. Everyone who stopped in for bacon and eggs or the local newspaper would see Jed as an expert on Linc's financial woes. Stopping at Clara's for coffee was the same as asking to be pumped for information.

"What did Jed have to say?" Sam asked. She tried to sound casual, but she hoped she'd get a hint of Jen's secret in this roundabout way.

Dad flashed her a don't-press-your-luck look, but answered, "Linc's gonna go down for this. No question. When a man builds his fortune on other folks' bad luck and hooks up with shady characters, the whole house of cards don't take long to collapse."

Sam nodded. Even though she'd never seen a house of cards, she imagined flimsy paper rectangles fluttering down, then blowing away.

Sam passed her written test with a score of 99 percent, still unsure how a driver should angle the car's wheels when parking on a hill. She didn't do as well on the driving portion of the test, but Dad swore to the examiner that Sam would only drive with a licensed driver in the next seat for months, or maybe years, to come, so Sam walked out of the office with a brand-new driver's license.

"I'd like to stop and celebrate, but I'm kinda antsy to get back home," Dad said, looking apologetic.

He didn't mention the coming baby, but Sam knew that was why, so she said, "Me too," though she felt a little melancholy at the thought of driving straight back as if they'd only been to town for groceries.

"There's a fast-food joint with a drive-through," Dad said as they left the Department of Motor

Vehicles' parking lot. "Guess we could get some milk shakes."

Sam turned toward Dad so quickly, her seat belt grabbed at her shoulder.

"You hate drive-throughs. Have you ever been in one?" she gasped.

"Don't like that closed-in feeling," Dad said, "but this one time probably won't kill me."

They were halfway home when Dad sucked in a breath between his teeth and shook his head.

"Almost forgot."

Sam closed her eyes and squeezed the paper cup with three pink sips left at the bottom so tightly, it crushed in her hand. She really, truly wasn't up for another surprise.

"There in the glove compartment is something from Trudy Allen. And Preston."

If it was something from Mrs. Allen, who'd opened the Blind Faith Mustang Sanctuary to rescue "unadoptable" mustangs the BLM would otherwise have destroyed, it couldn't be that bad, Sam thought. And though she'd gotten off on the wrong foot with Phineas Preston because he thought she'd stolen his palomino police horse, Sam had to admit he'd become kind of a hero to her.

Sam unfolded a piece of stiff gray paper. In a glance, she figured out she was holding a rough draft of a flyer Preston and Trudy planned to use for Blind

Faith Mustang Sanctuary's new program in which city people would pay to work with wild horses.

"Wild Horse Eco-Vacation," Sam read aloud from the typed portion of the page.

Dad made a weird sound and when she glanced at him, his mouth twisted as if he tasted something sour.

"I think that means ecology," Sam explained, then decided to read everything else silently.

Dad was an old-school rancher. To him, this idea smacked of a dude ranch.

It wasn't. Blind Faith Mustang Sanctuary needed money to pay vet bills and farriers, and to feed the captive wild horses. But Dad didn't see it that way. He thought of Mrs. Allen's Deerpath Ranch as a cattle operation and he'd known her husband, a serious cattleman like himself. Though Dad liked Preston and Trudy, and hoped they had a nice marriage, he couldn't see why anyone would take on caring for mustangs when they could mostly take care of themselves.

Sam turned the paper sideways to read notes made in Mrs. Allen's handwriting.

Deerpath Partners? Sanctuary Side-kicks? Wild Horse Helpers?

Apparently Mrs. Allen felt none of the names had the right ring for marketing to the public, because she'd put an *X* through each one. Sam had to agree. Maybe over winter break, she could help Mrs. Allen come up with some better ideas.

"Sorry I didn't show that to you sooner, seein' as how they need you Saturday."

"That's okay," Sam said. Going over to Mrs. Allen's house to help with the brochure would take her mind off the unpleasant things that seemed to be piling up around her.

"Trudy hasn't gotten much help. Preston's supplied some money and he's working on fences . . ."

Sam stared out the truck window as the landscape slipped by. She was interested in Mrs. Allen's program and what Dad had to say about it, but she couldn't escape thoughts of Norman White, helicopters, and Jake's voice saying, *Your friend ain't here no more.*

". . . high moisture content . . . good for the well . . . reinforce fence posts so the snow doesn't break it down . . ."

Sam nodded as Dad talked, but she was picturing the captive wild horses reacting to a helicopter overhead. Would they flash back to the day of their capture when the sky had been filled with a giant whirring insect? Could fence posts set in waterlogged ground be shoved over by the horses' charge for freedom?

"So even though they got the school district to help out, loaning them the bus and Pinkerton as driver and whatnot, for their pilot program—"

"Pilot?" Sam interrupted. The word snagged her attention.

"You know, sort of a first try," Dad said, as if she were simpleminded. "*That* kind of pilot program."

"Oh," Sam said with a sigh.

"Only a few kids were signed up because of it bein' so close to the holidays, and now they're worried the weather will keep some away, so I guess it don't matter much that I was slow in telling you they asked for your help."

"Wait," Sam said, "what do the holidays and weather have to do with writing the brochure?"

"Well, because it's not that at all. What I'm tryin' to tell you, honey, is they want you to launch the actual program—go with the bus to pick the kids up when they get in, then go back with 'em to Deerpath and, at least for day one, show those city kids how to partner up with wild horses."

"On Saturday? Day after tomorrow?" Sam asked.

"Isn't that what I said, Samantha?"

"I guess it is," she agreed.

"Honey, I'm not sure what's on your mind, besides the baby comin' and the usual wild horse troubles," Dad said as they turned onto the highway leading toward River Bend, "but you've only got one more day of school."

"I know, Dad," Sam said, "and school's really going pretty well."

"Well then, what I do when my brain's too doggone full to work right is make a list with two columns. One column's for things I have to do. The other's for things that just have to take care of themselves. Then, and mind you, it don't always work, I throw that second half away and try not to think about it."

"I'll give it a try, Dad," Sam said, and before she went to bed that night, that was exactly what she did.

Sam woke up ten minutes before her alarm clock went off. The storm Dad had been talking about last night must not have materialized. She didn't hear any wind. In fact, it was so quiet, the only thing she heard was the mumble of the kitchen radio as Gram prepared breakfast downstairs, the sound of the door as Gram called Blaze inside for a dog biscuit, and the thump of Cougar's paws as he jumped off her bed and rushed downstairs to find out why Blaze got a treat and he didn't.

Sam slipped out of bed and sat at her desk. She pulled her knees up under her flannel nightgown and spread the ruffled hem over her toes, then took one more look at the list she'd written out, sitting cross-legged on her bed the previous night.

CAN DO	CAN'T FIX
baby—study up on em. childbirth (!)	JEN !!!
Phantom's future /adopt? / college $ / BF?	Norman White's attitude

Winterizing chores	Kit's hand
Blind Faith program ***	Jake's an idiot

- HARP experience
- best present I can give wild horses is to make other kids love them
- once they see them, horses will stick to their hearts forever

The Can't Fix list was a lot shorter than the Can Do list. That was the good news, but why hadn't Jen called about the big secret?

"I'm sure she'll spill the beans tomorrow," Gram had said last night, but if that was supposed to be comforting, it hadn't been.

What if the good thing Jen and Lila had been excited about hadn't happened?

Sam scanned her list.

Norman White's attitude was a total loss, but the weather might stay so stormy, the helicopter pilots would refuse to fly. Except that could mean the horses couldn't find food, and this year's foals, most of them about Tempest's age, might starve. Sam picked up her pencil, but she didn't add that worry to her list.

Sam yawned. Not until yesterday, when Dad mentioned the possibility, had she worried that she might be the only one home when Brynna went into labor. Gram had books about all kinds of first aid, and there had to be something about helping someone have a baby. She knew it was a natural process. Dark Sunshine hadn't needed a bit of help, but people were more complicated than horses.

Last night she'd looked over her notes from Kit's interview because they were in the same notebook as her list. She was more convinced than ever that Kit loved rodeo so much that he'd go back to it the minute whatever injury that cast was hiding healed. Maybe then Jake would be himself again.

Why didn't Luke Ely, their dad, sit both guys down and talk to them? Maybe it was just something they had to work out, or Kit might not want to risk a major fight because he'd be leaving again so soon. Actually, she didn't care how their feud was resolved; she just hated Jake being mad at her.

For a guy who didn't use many words, he'd sure picked ones that hurt.

Sam tapped her pencil eraser on her desk and decided the best thing about making the list had been thinking about the Blind Faith program. The skills she'd picked up working with the HARP girls would help her with the city kids who came to the range already loving wild horses and wanting to help them. Her job, Sam decided, was to make sure the city kids got one glimpse of a herd running across the playa, free and wild. Then they'd stand up for the horses forever.

Sam's pondering came to an end when Blaze barked.

"Hush, you silly thing!" Gram's voice floated up the stairs between her footsteps.

Before Sam could ask why Gram was coming up to wake her before her alarm went off, Gram stood in the doorway in her red corduroy bathrobe and said something Sam had dreamed of hearing: "Snow day!" and then, before Sam could shout in celebration, Gram added two words that were even more beautiful. "School's canceled!"

Chapter Eleven

"What do you do on a snow day?" Sam asked Brynna as the entire family straggled down the stairs.

"Eat it, for one thing," Brynna said, licking her lips. "Mound fresh snow in a dish and drizzle it with maple syrup or orange juice."

"Oh, yum," Sam said.

"In town, you'd probably sleep in, but that's a waste of a holiday. Still, you can eat breakfast in your nightgown," Gram said.

"And wait for the pump to quit workin' because of a power failure," grumbled Dad, who was the only one already dressed.

"Oh, Wyatt, stop," Brynna said. She gave Dad a shove that made him smile.

Gram divided a huge cheese omelet and a stack of thick-sliced wheat toast among the four of them, promising Sam a bowl of snow with chocolate syrup after she'd had something that would "stick to her ribs."

Sam was licking the last bit of frozen chocolate from her bowl when she thought of more good luck brought by the snow.

"This means my teachers can't assign any last-minute homework. What I've got—just reading *Jane Eyre* for English and bringing in a baking sample for cooking class—is *all* I've got."

"Reading and baking," Dad grumped as if things had been tougher when he was a boy. "Sounds to me like you got off easy."

"Well," Sam stalled, certain Dad would fill her idle hours with work. "I probably wrote some other stuff down in my notebook and it's just slipped my mind."

"Fine," Dad said. He rose from the table, took his silverbelly Stetson from its hook, and placed it on his head. "Like I told you last night, winter weather brings new responsibilities. Don't forget."

"I won't," Sam promised, and she was even more relieved he hadn't piled on more chores when the phone rang.

"It must be Jen," Sam said, almost tripping on her nightgown as she skidded across the kitchen to grab the phone before anyone else could.

"Did you hear?" Jen yelled. "No school!"

"Yeah, but I'm mad at you—"

"Be mad at my parents. They're the ogres that—"

Sam heard sounds of lighthearted disagreement beyond her friend's voice.

"No, they're not ogres," Jen said. "I stand corrected. If they were, they wouldn't allow me to go on an exciting snow ride with you as soon as I do my chores."

Then Jen made a kissing sound. Sam assumed Jen had directed it at her parents, but that was a first. She couldn't wait to hear what had caused such joy at the Kenworthy household.

"Great," Sam said. "I have snow chores on top of my regular chores. I'm supposed to work with Dallas and Ross since Dad let Pepper go home to Idaho for the holidays."

Dad paused halfway out the door and turned around.

"Not that I'm complaining," Sam said, and she saw Dad nod before he kept going. "I'm supposed to keep all the buckets and troughs clear of ice, and the river where the cattle drink, too, if it gets frozen over—and, oh yeah . . ." Sam said the next part casually, wondering if Jen could hear her smile. "I'm also supposed to keep the road, from bridge to highway, shoveled off."

"What do they think you are, a snowplow? That's a huge job, especially if you can't drive."

Sam jiggled the phone cord, then swooped it like a jump rope, trying to make Jen guess her good news.

"Hello? I said . . ." Jen's voice trailed off in puzzlement.

"Well, actually . . . you'll never guess—"

"Get out!" Jen shouted.

"Yesterday my dad took me to get a hardship driver's license, and—"

"And you're not chauffeuring anyone anywhere, except for me, in case of emergency," Brynna reminded her.

"I know," Sam said.

"I heard," Jen said. "But Sam, that's amazing. Do you feel different? All old and responsible?"

"Not yet."

"Don't forget," Jen said solemnly, "we made a pact that neither of us would ever drive like Mrs. Allen."

"No way," Sam said. "But hey, since cars will never, ever replace horses in a sane world . . ."

"I hear you," Jen said. "I'll meet you at War Drum Flats as soon as I can."

Snow muffled everything. Edges of the bunkhouse, barn, and run-in shed were rounded off. At first Sam thought snow had already mounded into drifts, but then she realized the trees bowed toward the earth under their burden of snow, changed into smooth humps instead of tall slender things.

But it hadn't snowed any more since Dad had left the house. Sam followed his footsteps to the barn and to each water trough—none of which were frozen. She paused to shake the snow off the trees and they sprung up, sprinkling her with crystals as the branches reached for the sky once more.

The ice spangles on her sleeves melted into drops as she kicked down through the snow to the bare dirt in front of the chicken coops. The two roosters watched critically from their doorways before strutting out to scratch at the chicken feed she scattered. They didn't eat it, Sam noticed. They merely made chirring sounds that coaxed the hens to come out.

It was the perfect kind of snow, Sam thought—fluffy instead of icy. Deep, but not sticky enough to clump together on her boots and make walking impossible.

It was already warming up when she finished her chores and headed into the barn. She shed her jacket and hung it on a hook along with her long wool scarf before checking the creep feeder in Tempest's pen.

She smooched for the filly, but Tempest didn't come. Sam could hear her tiny hoofs galloping in her small pasture. Just as Sam emerged from the barn into the pasture, a slab of snow on the barn roof sloughed off and landed on Tempest.

The black filly reared, dumping the snow, then ran along the fence line, around and around, bucking and kicking until she made sure she'd outrun the cold white attacker.

"It's okay, baby," Sam crooned, moving toward the filly, but Tempest stood as far from the barn as she could, looking up at the roof, braced for another assault. "Want my glove?"

Sam yanked off a glove and dangled it, but the filly's trembling attention remained fixed far over Sam's head.

There was a lot to learn when you were a baby animal, Sam thought, and she couldn't teach Tempest what she should and shouldn't be afraid of. How could you anticipate something like a miniavalanche sliding off a rooftop?

Standing with hands on hips, waiting for Tempest to come to her for a comforting ear scratch, Sam glimpsed Dallas through the fence rails.

"What if I put Ace in here to keep her company after I come back from riding?" Sam called.

"Couldn't hurt," Dallas replied briefly, but Sam could tell he liked being asked.

Dallas had been on this ranch as long as Sam could remember. Dad claimed Dallas had forgotten more about horses than Dad had ever learned. Sam didn't always approve of Dallas's old-fashioned ways with horses, but he was kind at heart and he was the one who'd told her, just days after she'd come home from recovering in San Francisco, that she was born to the saddle.

"I think I will, then," Sam said, smiling, and went to get her tack.

The blanket of snow muffled the sound of Ace's hooves as he galloped. He snorted with each stride, sending plumes of vapor into the blue and white day, but that was the only sound Sam heard. The world was hushed around her, like the moment before a curtain goes up on a play.

Sam spotted Jen in her lime-green jacket on her palomino mare from at least a mile away, and they came together, horses circling each other in a whirlwind of white.

"Tell me!" Sam shouted, then cupped her gloved hands over her nose and mouth as she felt the cold burn her lungs.

"Harmony Ranch!" Jen shouted.

Jen's glasses were so fogged up, Sam couldn't see her eyes, and for one terrible moment she was afraid Jen was moving to ranch country far away.

"Ryan's taking over the Gold Dust and my family's entering into an official, on-paper partnership with him. It's going to be a cattle and palomino operation and we're all contributing something." Jen held her reins in her left hand as she counted off on her gloved right hand.

"Ryan's contributing the land and buildings, Dad's contributing his expertise and our breeding stock. Mom is kicking in her profit from the money she invested in her cousin's newspaper in Utah." Jen took a big breath. "And I'm contributing my college fund."

"Huh?" Sam asked. "I—how could you—?"

"Kind of a lot to take in, I know, but think of it this way: We all put in enough to split the whole ranch fifty-fifty."

"What about Linc and his financial mess?" Sam asked.

"Remember that fight Linc and Ryan had that day at the corral? When your friend Pam from San Francisco was here?"

"Sure," Sam said.

Pam had been visiting and they'd stopped by Gold Dust Ranch to bring Jen her homework because she was still recovering from an accident that had broken her ribs. Ryan had been working hard to recapture his Appaloosa mare Hotspot, and he and his father had quarreled about beef cattle, taking shortcuts and other things that had been hard to overhear from Jen's front porch.

"Apparently after that fight he deeded the Gold Dust to Ryan to teach him a lesson, so that he'd see it wasn't so easy to run a ranch—"

"No one ever teaches me a lesson by giving me a ranch," Sam mock-whined.

"I know," Jen sympathized. "But it's turning out so great. Ryan's willing to kind of treat Dad as a mentor and really run Gold Dust as a working ranch. Oh, and we've all agreed to change the name."

"To Harmony Ranch," Sam said slowly, but there was one thing in the torrent of information Jen had spouted that worried her. Sam swallowed, then asked, "Your college money?"

"It was a no-brainer," Jen said. "We all know I'm going to earn a scholarship that will get me into a good school."

From anyone else, it would have sounded like bragging, but from Jen it was simply the truth.

"Sure," Sam agreed.

"And the amount my parents have put away for me will help the ranch and, probably," Jen broke off to grimace, "won't go that far toward tuition at a really important college. So, I'm actually vested in the ranch."

"And that means?"

"As soon as I'm eighteen, I own a piece of it," Jen said, sighing. "Is that cool, or what?"

"Amazing," Sam said, "and so much better than my daydream, because this way you don't have to marry Ryan."

"I'm not ruling that out," Jen said, and when Sam gasped, Silly reared.

Looking orange against the snow, the palomino mare rocked back on her hind legs and pawed skyward with white stockinged forelegs.

Jen shifted her weight forward, brought the mare back down, and reined her in a prancing circle, then pointed at Sam. "That's about ten years in the future, and anything could happen between now and then. Besides, my parents might not want a convicted criminal blighting a branch of their family tree."

Sam laughed, then stopped as she realized Jen was studying her as if she were a specimen under a microscope.

"What?" she asked.

"You miss Jake."

"Miss him? That jerk? No, I don't. It hasn't been—"

"Call him and apologize," Jen suggested.

"For what?" Sam yelped. "I didn't do anything."

"There are always two sides," Jen began.

"Not this time," Sam told her.

"Well, you know he won't take the first step. Even if he's eaten up with regret, he's too shy to say so," Jen said.

"I don't care. He's the one who's wrong," Sam said. "How am *I* to blame for *him* being weirded out over his brother?"

"Kit? I thought he was great."

"He is," Sam insisted. "I think Jake's jealous or something."

There was a moment of silence. Silly played with the roller on her bit and Ace swished his tail and finally Jen sneered, "That sounds like him."

"What does?" Sam asked.

"Using you as his whipping boy."

Sam hesitated. She wasn't sure what that meant.

"You know, he takes out his resentment of his successful brother on you."

Sam wanted to tell Jen she was wrong, but when she remembered Jake's cold face, she couldn't. Then she told Jen the rest of it.

"I guess you're right. After all, he told me he was done being my friend. So, say what you want. I'm not going to defend him anymore."

"What a jerk. He always has been, Sam. You were just too nice to see it. Believe me, you're better off without him hanging around. He's such a loser."

"Now wait a minute," Sam snapped. "I know you guys have this rivalry, but Jake is always there when I need him. Like you. In fact"—Sam snatched a breath to keep going—"in fact, the two of you . . ." Sam's voice trailed off when she saw Jen's smug smile. "That was a trap, right?"

Jen had said all those rude things about Jake to see if she'd defend him, Sam thought. And it had worked.

"Just testing," Jen said.

"That wasn't very nice," Sam told her.

"I know, but you'll thank me for it later."

"No, I won't," Sam said, but she had to smother the laugh triggered by Jen's certainty.

"So, hey, in the meantime, until you forgive me?" Jen said, and Silly began prancing, attuned to the change in her rider's attitude.

"Yeah?" Sam said. Now Ace tossed his head and pulled at the bit in excitement.

"Catch me if you can!" Jen yelled.

She touched her heels to Silly's side, lined out across the snow-covered range, and Sam didn't even try not to follow.

When they finally stopped the horses, Sam could see the way up to the cleft in the mountains where the Phantom's secret valley lay. Covered with snow, the individual mesas were hard to make out. Only faint shadows indicated the plateaus. And when a wind fanned over the mountains and rushed over the snow, gathering cold before slamming into the girls and horses, Sam could see nothing up there but a curtain of white.

While Ace and Silly licked the snow at their feet, Jen studied the mountains, then steadied her glasses on the bridge of her nose.

"Something tells me that would be the perfect place for an avalanche," she said.

"What are you talking about?" Sam asked, rubbing her gloved hands over her numb cheeks, trying to stimulate a little feeling into them.

"When my mom was still home-schooling me, avalanches were something I wanted to study. You could say I got kind of obsessed with them. For instance, most people think that the most dangerous time for avalanches is in the spring, when the earth warms up and snow thaws and slides down."

Sam thought about the slab of snow that had slid down the barn roof onto Tempest that morning. "That's what I thought," Sam agreed.

"Well, it's true, but only by a few percentage points," Jen said. "And around here, if you're talking about naturally released avalanches, not something triggered by hikers, the time immediately after a storm, like during the first twenty-four hours—"

"Like now?" Sam asked.

"—is the most dangerous for blocking highways, smashing buildings, and stuff like that, and yeah, like now."

The wind moaned through the trees up on the ridge. Sam thought if she were the kind of person to imagine snow banshees, she might be shivering in her saddle. As it was, she knew she was only shivering because she was freezing.

"Look!" Jen said, pointing. "See that?"

"Give me a hint what I'm looking for," Sam said, squinting.

"The wind direction just changed. See, up there? Where it looks almost like white smoke swirling along the mountaintop?"

"Yeah," Sam said.

"That's because the wind is blowing up the far slope and down the closest one, scouring off snow from the other side and carrying it over the summit. What's really cool about that, though kind of dangerous, is that it could build up a cornice on this side."

"I don't know what that is," Sam admitted. "But it looks too light and powdery to be dangerous. I think you're joshing me, partner."

"Not at all," Jen said seriously. "A cornice is like, well . . . imagine a breaking wave. You know that top part where the crest kind of curls over? A cornice is like that, only it's built up of those 'light and powdery' layers of snow. And it freezes, but if it breaks off for some reason, it could start an avalanche."

Jen sighed, reveling in the wonders of science, but Sam just stared. Though the blowing snow didn't look scary to her, she didn't like the thought that a snow wave could be poised and ready to break, right where the Phantom and his herd felt safest.

Chapter Twelve

Overhead, the sky lay flat and white as a bedsheet, except for an ocher smudge of sun.

Returning from her ride, Sam listened to the tap of Ace's hooves on the cold earth and really looked at the road from the highway to the bridge over the La Charla River. Instead of just packed-down dirt, she saw two parallel paths with grass in the middle. The grass wasn't high. After all, trucks and cars mashed it down each time they passed, but today the grass stood up straight and white-tipped. Wheel marks on each side were filled with snowmelt that might have been water earlier in the day, but it had turned slushy now.

"It's probably close to freezing," Sam told Ace.

Her bay gelding flattened his ears, impatient to return to the warmth of the saddle herd.

"I've got a better deal for you than that," Sam told Ace. "If you're a good boy, you can spend the night in the barn with Tempest. She's in your old stall and pasture."

Ace's trot lengthened, and Sam kept studying the road. If that slush froze up, she'd have to remember to ride with extra care.

Dad and Ross had pulled off all of the horses' shoes for the winter because they believed "barefoot" hooves had better traction in mud and snow. But what about on ice? She'd read that police horses in cold cities had studded shoes to dig into the slick surface of the ice.

"If it gets that cold, we're not going out," Sam muttered to Ace, but the gelding gave a short-tempered swish of his tail as if he heard the hollowness of her promise. "Yeah," Sam said, rubbing the gelding's withers just in front of the saddle. "We both know if he needs us"—Sam glanced toward the Phantom's Calico Mountain home—"we'll ride out, no matter how cold it gets."

What if Norman White decided that the snowy range made it easier to spot wild horses and, on the bright cold days when there weren't storms—which was most days—he sent helicopters up to chase the horses into traps? Of course she'd go out and try to save the Phantom from captivity. He might have been her tame colt once, but he'd been a wild herd stallion for years now and she couldn't stand the idea that he would be rounded up, gelded, and sold to the highest bidder.

Sam spent the rest of her snow day logged onto the family computer. At the same time, she talked on the phone with Mrs. Allen and her fiancé, Preston.

Since they'd given Dad the gray paper flyer to show Sam, the couple had made progress planning and publicizing the program to raise funds and awareness for rescued wild horses.

"This is great," Sam said, watching their website take shape on the computer screen.

DREAM CATCHER WILD HORSE CAMP came alive as a montage of watercolor paintings, photographs, colorful lettering, and small blocks of information.

"I love the name and your artwork," Sam said. There was no sense mentioning how much more she loved Mrs. Allen's horse paintings than her portraits of carnivorous plants.

"And we used your photographs," Mrs. Allen pointed out.

Sam had noticed, of course, and she felt chills at how professional they'd made her snapshots look. In one, Mrs. Allen's grandson, Gabe, extended his hand to the colt he'd named Firefly. Another showed Callie, pierced nostril and all, playing her flute as wild horses grazed around her in the sanctuary field.

Sam's favorite was the photograph she'd shot of Faith, running through a summer pasture dotted with yellow dandelions. Most people looking at the picture wouldn't realize how brave the filly was, because she was totally blind and running into darkness.

"Hope we didn't presume too much, giving you a title."

Sam heard Preston's voice for the first time and realized the older couple must be talking from different phone extensions.

"Of course not, Phineas," Mrs. Allen scolded, "this was all Samantha's idea."

"You gave me a title?" Sam asked.

"Look on down the page," Preston told her.

Sam scanned past information on five- and ten-day school vacation sessions. She saw announcements for parent-child wild horse camps, church and school field trip details, and then, amid the contact information, she picked out her own name.

Samantha Forster, mustang mentor, she read, and maybe she made a little gasp, too, because Preston said, "Grammatically, I'm not sure that's right. It might mean you're mentoring the horses instead of the kids."

"That's perfectly all right," Mrs. Allen said. "She'll be mentoring both of them. And Samantha, I've talked with Grace about this, and I know you're busy with your own horses and school, and heaven knows every one of you Forsters will have your schedules turned upside down when the baby arrives, but we want you to be as much a part of our Dream Catcher program as you like."

"According to Trudy," Preston said, "she wouldn't be helping the wild horses if it weren't for you."

Sam's throat tightened. More than anything, she wanted to help the wild horses. And she'd actually done it. She wasn't finished, either.

She tried to joke past the surge of emotion. "Did she say whether I got the credit for that, or the blame?"

Preston chuckled and Mrs. Allen laughed before answering. "That's still under discussion."

"Now, about tomorrow," Preston said, refocusing the conversation. "We sent out a mailing—electronic and paper," he clarified proudly, "to about three hundred school counselors, 4H advisors, and tack shops, and posted links to our website every place we could think of, but with the holidays and bad weather, we'll only have three confirmed visitors."

"Maybe that's good, for the first camp," Sam suggested.

"That's just what I said. It will be our trial run," Mrs. Allen put in.

"There'll be a father and son from Topeka, Kansas, and a twelve-year-old girl, all on her own, from Pacific Pinnacles, California." As Preston went on, Sam heard echoes of the strict police lieutenant he'd been before retiring. She knew everything would be as organized as possible.

In minutes, Sam finished taking notes that told her to meet the school bus driven by Mr. Pinkerton, and ride it to the airport in Reno. There, she'd meet the three campers and accompany them back to Blind Faith Mustang Sanctuary.

"This first time, we'll just be putting them up in the house, like guests," Mrs. Allen said.

"And we're hoping, with your superior knowledge of the area, you can act as sort of a travel guide, pointing out local landmarks, wildlife, and so on," Preston said finally.

"It sounds great," Sam said.

"I had hoped to get Jake Ely to help you out with this," Mrs. Allen said, "but . . ." Her sigh gusted loudly into the phone.

But what? Sam wondered. She bit her lip, hoping Mrs. Allen would tell her what Jake had said, but she didn't. When Sam couldn't take the quiet on the line any longer, she said, "Don't worry. I can handle it alone."

The next morning, Sam woke to two entirely different words than she had the morning before.

"Cold snap," Dad said, rapping on her doorframe as he came down the hall.

It was still dark on the first Saturday of winter vacation. Sam didn't want to get up.

"'Kay," she told Dad, then scooted down farther

in her bed, burrowing under the warm blankets.

Nightmare, she told herself. She must be having a nightmare, because Dad wouldn't really clomp into her room, stand next to her bed, and romp her plush horse Jingles up and down her blanketed body.

Sam opened one eye and saw Dad's silhouette looming over her. She wasn't dreaming.

"Cold snap?" Sam mumbled without bothering to lift her head.

Dad brushed away the locks of auburn hair covering her face. His touch was gentle, and Sam wished he'd sit down on the bed and keep doing that, like he had when she was a child. That would be so cozy and comforting. He could sit there and stroke her forehead until she fell back to sleep.

With each heartbeat, Sam sank toward a second slumber.

"Listen, sleepyhead, I need your help," Dad said. "Until the ice is broken, no animal on this ranch will have water."

"No," Sam moaned, but her legs were already peddling under the covers, imagining the saddle horses licking the surface of their frozen trough and the range cattle stamping at the river, then falling in and dying of hypothermia because of her.

"I'm up," she said, and stood with her hands on the hips of her nightgown, weaving from side to side before she remembered to open her eyes. She stood there all alone. Not even Cougar was in her room.

Dad had known the combination of responsibility and guilt would get her going.

Without a thought for her appearance, Sam dressed in long underwear, wool pants, and a down jacket. She grabbed a pink knit cap to pull on under her old brown Stetson, a scarf, and her warmest gloves. The fuzzy mittens Gram had knitted for her were tempting, but with all the chores Dad had assigned her, she'd need the finger mobility of her waterproof gloves.

Downstairs, Blaze was curled up in front of the hearth. Dad had already built a fire.

Sam stood staring at the orange flames and listened to their cozy crackling. Why had he started a fire when no one would have time to enjoy it?

"We'll just keep it going," Dad said, leaning through from the kitchen. "We've got plenty of wood cut and stacked, and if there's a power failure, we'll be set. Besides, I'm hoping Brynna will sit right there and read, kind of take it easy on the couch all day."

Sam rolled her eyes, but not in envy.

That wasn't going to happen. Brynna hadn't been going to her office every morning, but that didn't mean she wasn't working. No corner of the house was safe from her dusting or polishing, and she'd started studying kitchen shelves, looking for things to throw away. Gram claimed Brynna was "nesting," and that it meant Brynna would deliver the baby soon.

But the baby wasn't due for two more weeks and, according to Brynna, she had no other symptoms indicating that labor would start sooner. She told Gram, nicely but firmly, that "nesting" was an urban legend.

"You mean it's an old wives' tale," Gram had said, "and you needn't pretty it up."

Brynna had laughed, so Sam didn't know if she'd heard Gram add, "But it's true, all the same."

Sam shook her head to make herself quit staring at the fire.

"Come on, boy," Sam called to Blaze.

Without opening his eyes, the Border collie gave two apologetic thumps of his tail and stayed where he was.

"I'm going to tell Singer you're a slacker," Sam told him, but Blaze simply rearranged his plumy tail to cover his nose.

Turning away from her dog, Sam wondered if Jake had brought Singer inside, to sleep in his room, or left him in his barn kennel. If things had been different, she might have called and asked.

When Sam entered the kitchen, Dad handed her a cup of sweetened, milky coffee. How early was it, she wondered, if Gram wasn't up yet? Just then she heard the floorboards overhead squeak, and she smiled. Gram was no slugabed.

"Drink it," Dad said, "and you can have breakfast later on. Right now we need to help the stock."

When Sam walked outside, she saw the surface of the snow was glazed with ice. It wasn't shiny, exactly, but the rising sun picked out ice crystals. They shone like long silver glitter, and in some places the crystals were multicolored.

The bundled figures of Ross, on his bald-faced bay Tank, and Dallas, on the rat-tailed Appaloosa Jeepers-Creepers, moved slowly toward the bridge.

Yesterday the snow had been silent underfoot. This morning it crunched and each of Sam's steps broke through to the softer snow underneath, wetting her past her boot tops.

As she walked past a tree she'd cleared off yesterday, she heard the snap of a twig. Then the ungrateful tree showered her with snow.

It was warmer inside the barn. Ace and Tempest crowded close, sharing their body heat and breathing excited puffs of hay breath as they followed Sam. They watched her use a short shovel to break the ice on the water in their small corral. Instead of shattering, the icy surface came loose in a gray disk. Sam held her breath and grabbed the big, flat ice cube with her gloved hands, then threw it onto the ground.

Immediately, Tempest went to investigate, pouncing like a cat at the new object, then sniffing it all over. Ace watched and yawned, showing Sam his long tongue.

"I wish I could stay and play with you," Sam said, giving her horse a one-armed hug, "but I can't."

Sam grabbed the iron digging bar Dad had told her to use to break up the river, and carried it along with the little shovel. The digging bar weighed over thirty pounds. After her boots slid on a slick patch of snow and she had to juggle both tools, she had a new admiration for the cowboys who'd done her jobs in years past.

She broke the ice off all of the troughs around the ranch yard. Then, raising the scarf she'd tied around her neck to cover her nose and mouth, Sam picked her way across the bridge boards. She was supposed to keep them safe and clear, but the bridge and the road to the highway had thawed enough that no snow covered them.

In fact, the road felt hard under her boot soles, as if the dirt had frozen. Grateful that there was no snow to shovel, Sam kept walking toward the river.

She dropped the shovel, grabbed the digging bar, and aimed it point-down toward the frozen surface. Ice flew up like shards of glass, so she kept repeating the up and down motion, ignoring her burning muscles.

Until she looked up, Sam thought the sound she heard was ice hitting the ground. Smiling, she realized she'd heard the clatter of hooves.

Alerted by the sound of her breaking the ice, the cattle came running, red coats bright against the gray morning. All the Herefords except one stopped, wide-eyed and wary, when Sam called, "Buddy!" at the sight of the young heifer who'd been her pet.

The cattle were thirsty, but they were ready to bolt if she did something else scary.

Used to Sam's voice, Buddy crowded past the others and lowered her curly white head to drink.

Sam didn't say another word, because she didn't want to spook the rest of the animals, but she grinned when Buddy stopped drinking and raised her head to stare at her.

Yeah, it's me, Sam thought as her breath and the heifer's combined in a mist between them.

Buddy's white eyelashes blinked. Then she tossed her slick pink nose, gave a storybook "moo," and kept drinking. To Sam, it meant "hi," but the rest of the cattle took the sound as a signal that Sam was harmless.

As Sam backed away from the river, the rest of the cattle pressed in to drink, too.

Suddenly, the iron digging bar weighed her arms down with heaviness she couldn't ignore and her cheeks burned hot. Or maybe cold. Since she couldn't tell which, Sam decided to return to the house and warm up before doing anything else.

As she walked back across the bridge, she saw light streaming from the barn and heard the faint sound of the tack-room radio.

Sam knew she should return the shovel and digging bar to the barn before going into the warm kitchen. She didn't want to. She'd been picturing herself just dropping the heavy tools by the porch, but she tramped past the house and the beckoning smell of hot cakes and bacon and tottered toward the barn.

She'd bet she hadn't been outside for even an hour. She could do it, she told herself, and a minute later, Dad's approval made the extra effort worth it.

At first he didn't look up, just considered the nylon halter he held and said, "Still like leather better, but can't fault these things for tough. Hardware gives out before the halter."

Sam leaned the shovel and digging bar in a corner and slapped her hands—chilled from the metal, even through her gloves—against her legs.

"They all glad to see you?" he asked.

Sam looked up to see silent praise in Dad's brown eyes.

"Yeah." She felt her frozen face reflecting his smile and realized this was what they both liked about ranching. On a good day, you got back what you put into it. She'd hated getting up in the dark and going out in the cold, but the animals had thanked her without words.

Dad nodded toward the radio. "Airport's open. No roads closed. Guess that means you'll be ridin' the bus in to pick up the kids for Trudy and Preston's—"

"Dream Catcher Camp," Sam said. The name gave her wonderful chills, almost as much as the title they'd given her.

"Right."

They both glanced up at a rustling sound in the rafters. Sam didn't see any pigeons, but they must have been up there.

"I'm going to go in and eat," Sam said, starting toward the barn door. "Shall I wait for you, Dad?"

"Be in soon," Dad said. "You go on."

She was probably imagining she could smell breakfast all the way out here, but the aroma drew Sam just the same. She took two steps before Dad said, "I'm proud of you for helpin' Trudy out."

"It's just a day or two, and I haven't done anything yet," Sam cautioned him.

She waved and started for the house.

Golden hot cakes and sizzling bacon. Her mouth watered and she didn't slow down, even when his voice reached her again.

"Soundin' more like a cowgirl every day, isn't she?" Dad asked, and Sam shook her head. Dad didn't make a habit of talking to himself.

Chapter Thirteen

The helicopter was out again, searching for horses, and Sam sat in a freezing-cold, nearly empty school bus with the one Dream Catcher Wild Horse camper who'd shown up. She might as well have been alone.

Sam pressed her forehead against the bus window, trying to see the chopper, but she couldn't. Only the vibration from its rotors told her it was out there.

"The men in that helicopter are looking for wild horses to round up and bring in for adoption," Sam explained to the girl sitting beside her.

The girl's small hands twitched on her book, a nonfiction volume about horses. She nodded, but she didn't look out the window or glance up from the page she was reading.

Sam sighed. This was about the tenth time she'd tried to get the kid to talk. Was Darby Carter incredibly shy or just rude?

At the last minute, a phone call from Mrs. Allen had told Sam that she'd only be meeting one Dream Catcher camper, the girl from California. Sam had actually thought that would be kind of cool. She'd seen herself making friends with Darby Carter of Pacific Pinnacles, California, by answering her questions and telling her fun things about wild horses. So far, they weren't even acquaintances, let alone friends.

The stick-thin girl with a long black ponytail had plodded down the airport corridor with lowered eyes, and no matter what Sam did, Darby answered with the fewest words possible.

The instant Darby had settled into her seat—Sam had offered Darby the one next to the window, but she'd shaken her head "no"—the girl had pulled the book from the pocket of her pink Windbreaker and snapped it open. She sat with her shoulders shrugged up high, almost covering her ears.

Probably so she won't hear a word I say and have to answer me, Sam thought.

With a sidelong glance, Sam noticed, again, how totally underdressed for the weather Darby was. Bony ankles showed between the hem of her jeans and her tennis shoes. The top she wore had short sleeves. Sam could see them right through the nylon

Windbreaker, and the sight made her shiver.

Darby might be from sunny southern California, but she was driving through the snow-covered desert in freezing temperatures. Mr. Pinkerton, the bus driver, must have noticed, too, because twice Sam had heard the bus's heater huff hotter. Not that the adjustment took the chill off the cavernous vehicle. The heater only magnified the smell of old sack lunches. Sam tried not to smell the bananas, peanut butter, and limp lettuce. If she'd only had herself to think about, she would have chosen cold over that odor.

"Are you warm enough?" Sam asked.

When Darby opened her mouth to answer, her teeth chattered.

"I have an idea," Sam said.

Walking carefully up to the front of the moving bus, aware of Mr. Pinkerton's eyes watching her in the mirror, Sam unzipped the plastic covering on the emergency blanket next to the first-aid kit clamped to the bus wall.

"Can I use this?" Sam asked, just to be polite.

"Sure," Mr. Pinkerton said. He'd been talkative on their way to the airport, but now that they were within twenty miles of Deerpath Ranch, he looked weary and sounded cranky as he added, "Don't know what's wrong with this radio." He gave it a thump. "Not that it matters. Everyone in the bus barn is on vacation. Except for me."

Over hissing static, Sam heard a beeping, and Mr. Pinkerton grumped that it was unlikely anyone would hear his transmissions except for bored citizens' band radio operators who got a kick out of eavesdropping on official conversations.

He probably couldn't wait to get rid of them, and Sam didn't blame him. Even as a brand-new driver, she knew the weather conditions made the road slippery.

Mr. Pinkerton had complained that though the fresh snow wasn't deep, there'd been that cold snap this morning and yesterday's snow had turned icy. He felt safer driving slowly, so it might take a long time to reach the ranch.

Sam figured as soon as he dropped her and Darby off at Blind Faith Mustang Sanctuary, he'd head for the warmth of Clara's coffee shop, where his girlfriend Junie worked as a waitress.

Sam touched each seat back for balance as she made her way back down the aisle toward Darby.

"There's some of those little heat packets in the first-aid kit, you know, the little disposable hand warmers?" Mr. Pinkerton said before Sam had gone too far. He reached up to open the metal clasp holding the kit closed. "Just save me one of them. I'm thinking I'll have to get out and put on the tire chains before we reach the ranch."

Sam started to turn back around, but Darby's protest stopped her.

"No, I don't need it," Darby said.

"If you're sure," Mr. Pinkerton said, and his hand dropped back to the steering wheel.

Sam shrugged and kept walking back to her seat.

Darby stifled a cough as Sam settled beside her and draped the blanket over their laps and legs.

Was Darby sick? Sam kept her eye on the girl. When she breathed, her chest seemed to draw in instead of swelling outward. And she was awfully pale.

"I bet you paid for this trip yourself, didn't you?" Sam blurted.

Darby couldn't help but react. Her head snapped to face Sam. Brown eyes that looked too big for her face stared at Sam as if she were psychic.

"How did you know?" she gasped. Her breath whistled a little as she did.

"You love horses," Sam said, pointing at the book, "and even though you have a cold or something, you still came."

Darby looked down at her book again and her cheeks colored for the first time.

"I'd do the same thing," Sam told her. "You wouldn't believe the things I've done for horses."

"Like what?" Darby asked in a rattly whisper.

This time when she coughed, Darby pressed her hand against her chest, trying to make herself stop. When she finally did, Sam thought Darby looked almost blue around the lips. That couldn't be good, but the girl was finally starting to open up, so Sam kept talking.

"Like, well . . ." Sam's first thoughts were of the Brahma bull, feral dogs, and a cougar. Put all together, it sounded pretty bad. "Uh, probably stuff I shouldn't tell you."

Darby's eyes lowered to her book. Her shoulders hunched up all over again.

Nice going, Sam told herself, then decided she'd tell. What did it matter? The kid lived somewhere near Hollywood, according to Preston. How likely was it that Darby would copy the crazy things she'd done?

"I sneak out at midnight to see this wild horse who's a friend of mine."

Darby kept reading.

"No, really," Sam told her. "He was my horse when I was little, but he, uh, got loose and now he's wild, but sometimes he comes back to visit."

Darby glanced up long enough to roll her eyes and say, "I'm twelve, not stupid."

Sam laughed out loud. She hadn't expected Darby to have a smart mouth once she opened it.

"I know it sounds far-fetched," Sam said, "but I'm telling you the truth."

It's amazing what love can do, Sam thought, but the words were too sappy to say. Instead, she searched the landscape for her horse, just as she'd been doing all week.

"I keep"—Sam pressed her face against the freezing glass again—"thinking I might see him, but most wild horses have gone to shelter. I probably won't see him again until spring."

"What about the helicopter?"

So she *had* been listening.

"The pilots fly back over the canyons and scare them out into the open," Sam said. "I'd like for you to see some mustangs in the wild, before we get to the ranch, but if they're run into a trap and captured—"

"Here come a bunch," Mr. Pinkerton muttered. He didn't sound happy about it.

A memory flickered through Sam's mind, of the time Mr. Pinkerton had reported her to the principal for getting off the bus and going to the Phantom. This time, Sam felt a lurch as the bus driver took his foot off the gas pedal. Because of the icy road, he was trying to slow down without slamming on the brakes.

"I see them! I do!" Darby pointed across the aisle through the windows. Sam saw them, too.

Holding on to the backs of the seats for balance, they crossed to the other side of the bus.

"Sit down," Mr. Pinkerton snapped, and they did.

Spike and Yellow Tail bounded over the frozen range.

"Are they playing?" Darby asked.

At first they did look playful, but then Sam noticed the horses' wide-open mouths and the dark patches of sweat marking their coats.

"They're tired. And out of breath," Sam said. "The helicopter is pushing them pretty hard."

"Pushing them where?" Darby asked.

"I don't know." Her own words set off a surge of fear, and Sam ducked down so that she could see out each window. The helicopter had to be aiming the young stallions somewhere, but the closest trap she could think of was at Lost Canyon, and the horses were headed in the wrong direction for that.

Then, the helicopter raised higher off the snowy range and buzzed ahead of the horses. Its roar sounded above the bus as it crossed the highway.

"I think he's trying to turn them," Sam said.

"No," Darby whispered.

Sam glanced over to see that Darby's knuckles were pressed against her mouth.

As the helicopter stopped herding them, Spike skidded to a stop. Bay haunches tucked like a roping horse, he threw up clots of snow and halted short of the road, then swung around and galloped west. *Back toward the trap,* Sam thought, sighing.

But the golden chestnut kept coming. Yellow Tail's hooves seemed to float above the snow and he didn't hesitate. Full of his own speed, he galloped on. Even when the helicopter passed over his head, pursuing Spike, the stallion thought of nothing but running.

If he kept coming, the bus and the horse would collide!

"Stop!" Sam screamed.

There was no squeal of brakes. The bus tires hissed.

Sam grabbed the seat in front of her and stared out the windshield. She saw Mr. Pinkerton's hands fly on the steering wheel. Out of the windshield she saw only white. Something fell clanging inside the bus. She and Darby ducked instinctively, but nothing hit them before the *boom*.

Scraping, tipping, falling across the aisle, hitting her knee, shoulder striking metal, hearing a sound like a garbage can rolling in a high wind—and then, suddenly, they stopped.

Dizzy, head spinning though her body wasn't, Sam opened her eyes. She swallowed to keep back the nausea threatening to make her vomit.

At first, what Sam saw didn't make sense. A skylight? And a bundle lay on top of her.

It moved.

Sam flinched from whatever it was, until she heard harsh breathing that wasn't hers.

Darby. She was in the bus with Darby, a frail twelve-year-old. She was supposed to be in charge. The mustang mentor. And the bus had—what? Rolled over? Hit the stallion? Run off the road into a ditch?

That wasn't a skylight overhead, Sam realized. Those were the windows. The bus had rolled, but not far. It lay on its side.

"Sam?"

With a shivery laugh, Sam knew she'd never been so glad to hear her own name.

"I'm here. Darby, where are you?"

Bony elbows and knees told Sam more quickly than words that the bundle atop her was Darby.

"Don't move for a minute," Sam said.

"At least the horses—" Darby gasped, not finishing the sentence. She started another one. "I've never seen snow 'til today, or ridden a horse. Ever."

"Are you okay?" Sam asked, because the girl really wasn't making sense.

"Hawaii, where her family—*my* family's there! So, I haven't told my mom I love her, not since last New Year's. That was my New Year's resolution, have you ever heard of anything so mean? But I—"

"Darby!" Sam snapped the name, even as she wondered why she hadn't heard Mr. Pinkerton's voice yet.

Darby was wheezing. Was her chest crushed? Sam thought of Gabe trapped in a car. Nothing on *her* hurt, and Darby wasn't crying, but she was still gasping out disconnected words. Maybe they made no sense because Darby didn't have the breath to pronounce each word loudly enough to be heard.

"—because she's an actress. Not a very good one, but she won't go home to the islands. That's what she always says. Never go back to Kamuela, but I want to go. I *have* to go. Who else do you know that's descended from paniolo horse charmers?"

Sam hoped it was relief that made the other girl talk such nonsense. That would be a lot better than a head injury.

But Darby could be delirious. Whatever was wrong, she couldn't breathe. Sam felt Darby's small body arch, trying to suck in a breath.

"Stop talking."

"I—"

"No. I mean it, Darby. Don't talk. Just breathe."

Darby quit babbling, but she thrashed around as if searching for something, and then—

What was that sound? Sam felt chills on her nape. What was fizzing? Or spraying? Was something on the bus about to explode?

"What *was* that?" Sam asked. "Darby?" Sam really wanted a second opinion, because suddenly she was thinking of snakes. They couldn't live in snow, of course, but what if one had lain curled up in some warm niche in the bus until the tumbling shook it loose?

"My medicine," Darby wheezed. "That sound was my inhaler. I have asthma."

Of course you do, Sam thought, going limp with relief. *How dumb am I?*

Instead of saying that, though, Sam called out, "Mr. Pinkerton?"

He didn't answer and the silence unsettled Darby even more.

"I've gotta get out of here," Darby said anxiously. "I want my mom."

"You'll get your mom," Sam assured her, pushing away thoughts of her own mother.

Cowgirl up.

Sam reminded herself she was in charge whether she wanted to be or not. At least it wasn't dark. It was the middle of the day. Things only looked strange because she was sideways in the bus, just like the creepy bus in the ravine.

"Are all buses basically unstable?" Sam wondered aloud.

"Sure they are," Darby said as if she really knew. "That's why it's illogical that they don't have seat belts, but for fish-cal reasons they don't. They want to shove in as many kids as possible."

Darby had sounded a lot like Jen, until she got to that one word.

Sam asked, "What's fish-cal?"

"Maybe that's not how you say it," Darby said, sounding embarrassed. "It's spelled f-i-s-c-a-l. I'm not sure. It's just . . ." Darby's voice hushed softer with each word. "I read more than I talk."

The girl sounded like she might cry.

"Who cares?" Sam said. "Right now, I want you to think about all your body parts."

"My *body* parts?" Darby's tone had shifted. Now she sounded like she might burst into giggles.

"Does anything hurt? Think," Sam insisted.

It was quiet for a few seconds. Then, Darby said, "My knees."

"Mine, too. I think we fell on them, against the floor of the bus, when it rolled."

"Okay. That's why everything's"—Darby made a kind of hiccup—"sideways."

"Yep, that's why," Sam agreed, as she felt sensibility returning. "Now, I'm pretty sure Mr. Pinkerton's just unconscious, but we've got to check and see if we can help him. Okay?"

"Okay."

"And then we'll get out of here. Can you—if you're sure you're not hurt—reach something and pull yourself off of me?"

"Yeah," Darby said, and then, as simply as if Sam had told her to blink, she did it.

Sam sighed in relief. The girl was little, but still.

With a minimum of flailing around, Darby swarmed over the seat in front of them and disappeared.

Sam sat up and called after her, "What can you see?"

"Blood," Darby gasped. "There's blood on the bus driver's head and he's not moving."

Chapter Fourteen

It took Sam a few seconds to get her bearings.

Like a carnival fun house with furniture nailed to the ceiling to make you feel like your world has turned upside down, the rolled-over bus disoriented her. Sam found herself planting her feet sideways to climb the aisle between the seats. Only the seats kept her from falling back down to the windows that ran along the right side of the bus, and the gaps between the seats were scary.

Darby, though, scampered like a monkey, beating Sam down the aisle to Mr. Pinkerton by a full minute.

"He's alive," Darby said, moving the hand she'd held in front of the man's nose and mouth.

"Just resting," Mr. Pinkerton sighed, but his eyes didn't open.

Together, the girls looked up for the first-aid kit. It wasn't above the big front windshield where it had been before.

When Sam found it on the floor, she was relieved to see it hadn't opened and spilled the sterile gauze and bandages. She realized, though, looking at the cut on Mr. Pinkerton's head, that the first-aid kit had probably made the wound.

That was what her last year's English teacher, Miss Finch, would have called ironic, Sam thought. She remembered Mr. Pinkerton reaching up to unlatch the kit to get the hand-warming packets. He must have loosened it from its clamp.

Head wounds were supposed to bleed profusely, but only a trickle of blood streaked down from Mr. Pinkerton's receding hairline, and it took the girls just a few minutes to clean the cut and tape a gauze pad in place.

They covered him with the emergency blanket, then Sam stared into the first-aid kit, looking for anything else that could be useful. The scissors? Maybe. Antibacterial cream? No. What was that? She took out a roll of something that was as bright yellow as crime-scene tape, but spongy.

"Sports wrap," Sam said, recognizing the stuff she'd used to bind an ankle she'd sprained playing basketball.

Mind spinning, Sam pocketed the big roll, thinking she might use it later. Once she got out of the bus, she could tie it on bushes to attract attention. Or something like that.

"Thanks, girls," Mr. Pinkerton said. "I can't seem to clear my head. Give me a minute."

"Just rest and I'll go for help," Sam told him. "Darby will stay here with you." She waited for a response, but none came. "Mr. Pinkerton?"

"Keep drifting," he apologized. "That helicopter should be back, though."

If the pilot saw us crash, Sam thought.

If he looked back from chasing Spike.

If he hadn't already landed at some remote capture site where he had other horses penned and ready to be trucked to Willow Springs Wild Horse Center.

"Yep," Sam said in what she hoped was an upbeat tone, but she felt Darby watching her. Oh, well. Whether the younger girl could see her skepticism or not, Darby had a job to do while Sam hiked for help. "You're supposed to keep people with head injuries awake, so talk to him. Okay?"

Darby swallowed and gave Mr. Pinkerton a sidelong glance.

"Okay?" Sam repeated, and Darby nodded.

Sam pulled her gloves out of her pocket, ignoring the shower of other stuff—bits of granola bar, a pencil, and general pocket fluff—that came with them. Then she put them on.

Sam considered her clothes and boots and decided she was already bundled up against the cold.

This was as good as it was going to get. Now she was just wasting time.

"I'm out of here," Sam said. "If you want, keep trying the radio."

Darby nodded.

Sam wrapped her hands around the pole next to the front stairwell and started to climb down. The door was closed.

No problem. She'd seen Mr. Pinkerton open and close this door a thousand times.

Sam reached for the lever and pulled. The lever moved, but the door was jammed against a crust of snow. She pushed harder. She tried it six times, but some snow-covered rock or ridge of dirt blocked the door from opening more than a few inches.

Sam glanced at Darby, partly because the girl had begun breathing hard again, partly with a ridiculous hope that Darby was small enough to squeeze out. But there was no chance she could stick more than one skinny arm through that opening. Even if she could, once Darby got outside, she wouldn't know where to go.

Staring through the slanted windshield, Sam realized she wasn't even sure where they were.

"Okay." Sam kept her voice level. "That's why there's a rear exit. We'll be right back," Sam told Mr. Pinkerton. His vague smile told Sam she'd better hurry and get him some help.

The girls made their way to the back of the bus.

Sam didn't waste a second hesitating. She leaned on the Open Only in Case of Emergency lever.

"It won't open," Darby said fatalistically.

"Don't be silly. It's just not used much," Sam said, grunting with effort as she leaned on the lever. "It's sticking, but—"

"No, look." Darby pointed to a caved-in spot in the bus. Could a fender turn inside out? Sam thought of the scraping sound and the racket that had sounded like a garbage can blowing in the wind.

"Okay," Sam said again. "It could be a lot worse. That could have folded in on us."

"But how are we going to get out?" Darby whispered.

Sam's sensible side said they could wait for help. They were trapped, but they were trapped inside a big yellow-orange bus, in the middle of a highway, with enough gasoline to keep the heater running for a while. It was unlikely they'd use up all the oxygen in here. Impossible, in fact, because this vehicle wasn't exactly airtight. She remembered sitting next to Jen one day last year, with rain seeping in through the window next to them.

A smothered shriek came from the front of the bus. It didn't sound human.

"What's wrong?" Sam crab-stepped rapidly toward Mr. Pinkerton. It was like climbing Mount Everest sideways. Now she and Darby were both panting.

"The windows kick out," Mr. Pinkerton said.

His eyes were open. They looked directly into Sam's. He'd obviously been listening to them struggle to escape, and he had a solution. Had he made that frightening sound just to snag their attention?

"We'll try that," Sam said.

"The uphill ones," Darby said, pointing. Then she bit her lip. "Don't you think?"

"Yeah," Sam said, and they did it together, bracing, and using the impact of their soles. It didn't work the first time, or the second, but the third time they both gave tremendous shouts and thrust out with all the power in their legs. At last the window loosened at one corner.

Sam finished kicking it out. The blast of wind, laced with snowflakes, felt refreshing, but only for a minute. After that, she knew it would be a long, cold walk for help.

"You stay here," Sam said.

"Please, just for a minute. I've got to get out, but I promise I'll come back to him."

Darby's huge brown eyes pleaded and Sam gave in.

"Let's stay here for a minute, so I can figure out exactly where we are," Sam said, sitting on the freezing-cold side of the bus to look around.

Down the highway in front of them, she saw the turnoff to Willow Springs Wild Horse Center. She could walk that far, no problem, but there were miles of uphill, rutted road before it plunged down to the

BLM offices. The way would be treacherous and icy and there was rarely traffic in and out.

Walking the other way, into Lost Canyon, wouldn't help. There was a chance she'd encounter a truck full of captured horses driving toward Willow Springs, but her best bet was probably walking along the highway, toward Alkali.

It was about seven miles to Clara's coffee shop, but somebody would have to drive past before then, wouldn't they?

"Shouldn't you stay with the bus?" Darby asked.

Sam didn't answer. She wasn't sure.

Together they slid down the side of the bus and Sam hoped Darby could get back up and through the window to check on Mr. Pinkerton.

She was reminding herself that the girl could climb like a monkey, when that awful strangled scream came again. Suddenly, Sam knew it hadn't been Mr. Pinkerton.

The bus had hit Yellow Tail.

Hooves flayed against snow. A silken tail spread behind wet golden haunches.

"Oh!" Darby gasped.

Sam spared her a single glance and saw Darby's arms wrapped around her chest.

"Stay back," she ordered the younger girl, and Sam crept closer.

Please don't let the tire be on him, Sam prayed. *What will I do if he's dying?*

Don't lose it, she told herself, then circled wide around the horse and the front of the bus. Looking carefully, analyzing with her head instead of her heart, she made out what had happened.

The bus had grazed the stallion, then veered right. The horse lay where he'd fallen. And though there were swooping marks in the snow where his legs had thrashed back and forth, she saw no blood.

Maybe the bus fender had hit his other side. The damage could be hidden.

Sam fought the pain in her heart. Except for his coloring, he looked just like the Phantom—fine-boned Arab head, full mane and tail, a wide chest that would deepen as he grew up. *If* he grew up.

Stop it. Check out his legs. None of them seemed to be broken. Long and fleet, they might have turned him away from the worst of the impact at the last moment.

Suddenly Sam realized why Yellow Tail looked more streamlined and smaller than he had before.

This horse wasn't Yellow Tail. She was a filly with a white star on her chest.

"Help him," Darby whimpered.

Her voice stirred the horse into a renewed effort to rise. She plunged her forelegs forward. Her head lashed around, teeth bared as she glared through clumps of pale mane and forelock. Then she collapsed, head flat against the snow, panting openmouthed with nostrils red and distended.

Sam held her finger to her lips, then she whispered into Darby's ear, "She's wild. We scare her. Stay back and don't talk."

"I thought you said . . ." Darby's whisper trailed off.

"I was wrong," Sam admitted. "She's a filly. A little girl horse, and she needs help, too."

Darby obviously ached from knowing her voice had frightened the horse. She held both fists against her mouth, pressing so hard that her hands and face were white.

For a second, Sam was torn. If she stayed, she might help the horse, but how much? She needed a vet, and even then— She sighed. Touching was trauma to a wild creature. That's what Dr. Scott had told her. Human hands could hurt rather than heal.

Sam looked at Darby. With the suddenness of a slap, she realized the younger girl looked faint. Her skin was not just pale; it was translucent, sort of watery. Her black hair, wet by falling snow, was flattened against her small head.

She looks like a half-drowned kitten, Sam thought, *but she's a lot like me. Her heart is breaking for a horse. She would do anything to help her.*

Leaning close to Darby once more, Sam whispered the only words she could think of to comfort her. "We have a really great vet. He works with wild horses and he travels this road all the time."

Darby nodded frantically.

Leaving, Sam gestured toward the bus, but she

didn't watch to make sure Darby went back inside where it was warmer. She didn't have time to force her, so what was the point?

Sam strode toward Alkali, keeping to the edge of the highway. Two, or maybe three lives depended on help getting here right away.

She only glanced back once, then shook her head. She wanted to shout for Darby to back away from the mustang, to go check on Mr. Pinkerton, but seeing the way the girl hung over the injured filly, drinking her in with her eyes, Sam knew it would do no good.

Chapter Fifteen

Sam glanced at her watch. It was two o'clock in the afternoon. She decided to jog for ten minutes, which would be a pain in these boots, but that should put her, even in the snow, about a mile past the bus. Or wait, no—she'd keep going until she reached that stand of five trees up ahead.

Then she'd stamp an SOS in the snow and roll out the yellow tape and weight it with rocks. She'd keep walking, but surely she'd see someone by then.

She didn't. It was as if everyone between Oregon and California detoured around the state of Nevada.

Sam was muttering and puffing so loudly, at first she didn't hear the horn. Then she looked back, as she'd been doing about every ten steps anyway, and there sat Mrs. Allen's truck, like a tangerine-colored pup next to the orange bus.

Sam turned around and started jogging back.

She heard the helicopter and saw it hover over the crash.

Running and shouting at the same time, Sam yelled, "Get away!"

She heard other voices doing the same, ordering the helicopter to get away because it would terrify the injured horse. At least she hoped that was why, Sam thought, panting. She hoped they weren't beckoning the helicopter to land and help Mr. Pinkerton or Darby.

The chopper pulled up and headed her way. As it swooped overhead, Sam saw someone give her a thumbs-up and she was really afraid it was Norman White.

Oh, please, she thought, *let someone else come for the injured mustang. Not him.*

The sun turned the snow the color of golden sand and the five trees cast blue shadows, pointing back toward the bus. Sam felt light-headed and she told herself off for being a tenderfoot.

She should have eaten something before setting out for Alkali, or at least had a sip of the bottled water that was shrink-wrapped in the back of the bus near the emergency door. She hadn't even realized she'd seen it until now.

She swallowed and kept moving, but her ankles

felt like rubber by the time Preston stomped out to meet her. Gray-haired and athletic, looking every inch a cop—and not a retired one, either—he called out, "Doin' okay?"

"Fine," Sam said, but she probably would have been more convincing if her right foot hadn't crossed in front of her left and tripped her.

Gloves flat on the snow as if she were doing a push-up, Sam was struggling to her feet when Preston reached her.

"Rest a minute," Preston said.

It was a good idea. Sam's spinning head took a few seconds to return to normal. Eventually she pulled herself into a sitting position and asked, "Are they all okay?"

"Pinkerton and the kid are fine," he said.

"The horse?"

Preston shook his head. "We need Dr. Scott to check her over. I don't see why she's not up and gone. Must be that girl. . . ."

"Darby?" Sam coaxed.

"I know her name. It's what she's doing that's got me stumped." Preston stopped talking to let out a whoosh of air. "In police work, I've seen people who claimed to be psychics, who pretended to channel spirits—human and animal—but they were all frauds. This kid—Sam, what's the deal with her?"

Okay. Now it was time to get up and see what was going on. Darby had been a little weird, but not outlandish enough to baffle an experienced cop.

Sam looked past him, but she couldn't believe her eyes, so she walked closer, joining Mrs. Allen and Mr. Pinkerton, who were both keeping their distance from the filly.

The horse was still down. She was covered with a blanket that rose and fell with her breathing. So Darby had scrambled back inside to get the blanket. That was good thinking, but not strange.

Sam shook her head and looked around, scanning the area for Darby.

"I don't understand," Sam said as Preston moved to stand beside her, but then her mind registered what she'd seen.

Sam looked back.

The blanket was spread over the horse, but at the very edge of it, she'd glimpsed something else.

Lying in the snow beside the stallion, barely covered with an edge of blanket, lay Darby.

"Is she okay?" Sam asked Preston without looking away.

"Fine, except that she pretty much growled at the rest of us to get back."

Growled, Sam thought. It was a strong word, but she thought of the Phantom, unconscious and burned in a range fire. Jake had been forced to drag her away from him.

"It's been a while since my kids were that age, and I haven't done much work with abnormal juveniles,"

Preston went on, "but I'm pretty sure she's . . ." Preston shook his head and Sam wondered if he was reconsidering the pitfalls of the Dream Catcher program.

"Different?" Sam put in.

Preston answered, but Sam had stopped listening. All her attention focused on Darby.

The twelve-year-old was curled up, knees to chest, no more than five feet from the mustang's head.

No, she must be even closer, Sam thought, because one of Darby's small hands was outflung toward the filly, and vapor fogged the inches between the hand and the chestnut filly's nostrils. The horse breathed in and out, learning her scent, eyes watching her with something other than fear.

Would I try that with the Phantom? Sam asked herself. *Maybe, but he's my horse.*

Darby's weird jabbering about a Hawaiian horse charmer in her family tree hadn't made any sense, but neither did the bizarre scene before her.

"Did she say she'd had some kind of, shoot, I don't know, *experience* working with a vet or, uh, there was nothing in her application, but has she worked with abused animals?" Preston asked.

"She didn't talk much," Sam admitted, "but she told me she'd never ridden a horse in her life, only read about them. I think she reads a lot."

"Hope she's read about hypothermia, because that's what we'll be treating her for, soon as we can get her up and out of here," Preston muttered.

He stared across the snow, rippled now from the afternoon winds, as a white BLM truck came toward them.

"Norman White?" he asked Sam, and when she nodded, his mouth quirked in a half-smile. "Let's see if Trudy can handle him as well as she said she could."

It turned out Mrs. Allen handled Norman White just fine. She persuaded him to have the filly sedated and trucked to Deerpath Ranch, with the understanding that she'd be getting two orphan foals as well.

"We take all the care we can," she'd heard Norman say nervously, "but the herd we just brought in, well, some of the foals didn't mother up."

"Which herd?" Sam had asked. "What did they look like?"

"Not your precious white stallion's bunch," Norman had said, patting her shoulder.

Not the Phantom, but more wild horses had been taken from their homes and shoved into crowded corrals.

Sam began shivering, then edged away from Norman White and squatted close enough to talk to Darby. The girl was half turned away, using her inhaler, but when she was finished, she started whispering to Sam.

"All I could think to do was tell her stories, because I didn't want to sound like I was being all sorry for her, you know? So I told her some of the Hawaiian tales from my mom and she seemed to like them, as long as I didn't try to touch her head."

It was on the tip of Sam's tongue to ask Darby if she was loony or magical, but she was too humbled to do either.

"You did great," Sam said.

The mustang tossed her head at the sound of Sam's voice. Golden lips pulled back, she bared her teeth until Sam retreated a few steps. Then the filly let her head fall and she huffed loudly until Darby returned and lay quietly beside her once more.

Unbelievable, Sam thought. After everything settled down, she couldn't wait to go over to the ranch, sit down with Darby, and hear how she'd done it.

Because there wasn't room for her in the tangerine truck, Sam waited with Norman White and Mr. Pinkerton until a huge tow truck arrived that winched the bus out of the ditch and back onto the highway.

Mr. Pinkerton turned down Norman's offer of a ride to the county hospital in favor of sitting next to the tow truck driver who promised to drop him off for a late lunch at Clara's coffee shop.

But Sam had no choice. She had to allow Norman to drive her home.

They rode along in silence. She didn't know what he was thinking about, but Sam knew Brynna and Dad would hate thanking Norman for his neighborliness.

He was so quiet, Sam thought he was probably equally uncomfortable, too. Usually, she'd be polite and summon up words to smooth over the awkwardness. But not this time.

When Sam thought of Norman's single-minded desire to cage Nevada's wild horses, she didn't even try.

In her restless dreams, Sam wore huge thigh-high boots, carried a heavy backpack, and hiked in deep snow, passing Darby on the golden filly, Kit driving a carriage pulled by Witch, and Jake following them and falling behind because he was carrying Brynna, but dropping her time and again because somehow, in this nightmare, Jake was the one with a broken arm.

Vaguely, Sam realized she was really home in bed. Sometimes when she half woke, her face felt hot, and she remembered Gram saying that she'd gotten sunburned from the glare off the snow. Other times she surfaced enough to feel Cougar burrowing under her covers. He wasn't purring. He pushed at her shoulder, ribs, and ankles, making places for himself as if this was one big cat bed and he'd like her to move out.

The next morning a faint dusting of snow covered the ranch, but it felt warmer than it had the day before. It took only minutes to crunch up the ice that covered the animals' water, and as Sam walked out to check the river, she thought she'd carry the digging bar over her shoulder, just for practice.

The instant she tried to raise the bar to shoulder level, the muscles she'd strained tumbling through the bus screamed in protest.

Bad idea, Sam thought, and though she'd glossed over the accident as much as she could, she knew Gram would be on the phone this morning with Mrs. Allen. The good news was that Dad was staying close to the ranch and keeping an eye on Brynna. He wouldn't be stopping by Clara's and run into Mr. Pinkerton, who'd probably be brushing off the cut on his head as no big deal while he talked about the crash. At some point that would all come up, and Sam would explain everything as well as she could, but right now she wanted to get back to normal.

The morning was serene and she was following the delicate vee of bird tracks, wondering if birds' little feet got cold, when she was distracted by the paw prints of some small animal with a tail. Curious and determined to unmask the mystery animal, Sam was stepping as carefully as she could, accommodating her sore muscles and the iron bar, when the snow prints ended in a splatter of blood and a blot of wings.

"A hawk got something," Sam told Blaze, who'd followed her this morning, but she couldn't stop staring at the story in the snow.

Had the pawed creature heard the hawk coming? Had its head jerked up at the faint whistle of wind in feathers just before the impact?

She looked back over her shoulder. Obviously she had nothing to fear from a hawk, but she was thinking of the cougar that had attacked her. She hadn't heard it coming, but in a split second before it crashed into her back, she'd caught a smell just like dirty laundry.

There was nothing behind her. Blaze would have alerted her if there had been, but Sam was convinced that once you'd been stalked and set upon, been the prey instead of the hunter, you never got over it.

When Sam crossed the river, hurrying toward breakfast, she saw Ross using a square-nosed shovel to chip at the icy ruts over the bridge.

Ross was the biggest cowboy on River Bend Ranch, and the quietest. Although he and Sam had become friendly when he'd swept Jen off to the hospital after she'd been gored by a bull, and after Ross had shown Sam poetry he'd written about the Phantom, the big cowboy was still painfully shy.

Now, for instance, he looked up as if he'd done something wrong when Sam said, "I'm supposed to do that. Not that I had my heart set on shoveling." A smile struggled to form on her frozen face.

"Bored," Ross told her. "Wyatt said not to ride out."

"Oh. Well then"—Sam felt a celebration coming on—"thank you!"

With a nod, Ross returned to shoveling and Sam would have skipped back to the house if every muscle fiber in her body hadn't warned against it.

That job would have taken her at least an hour, and now she'd have more time to spend with Tempest—although the filly didn't seem heartbroken over her mother's absence.

Maybe, Sam thought, she should do something nice for Ross. After all, he must feel lonely with Christmas coming on and his family far away.

Too bad Pepper wasn't here, Sam thought, stamping her boots on the porch. Not only would he have filled out the bunkhouse Christmas, but yesterday's mail had brought something he'd absolutely love to see.

Inez Garcia, the Hollywood horse trainer who'd brought her stallion Bayfire to River Bend, had sent the Forsters the long, uncut first version of the movie that had been partially shot in Lost Canyon.

Okay, only an hour of it had been shot in Lost Canyon, but it starred Ace and Violette Lee.

Sam only cared about Ace, but Pepper had had stars in his eyes from the moment Violette Lee had arrived. Even when the actress proved to be stubborn and full of herself, Pepper didn't care. He'd called it the luckiest day of his life when he'd been on the spot to carry the actress off a plateau and drive her to the hospital for a checkup on a sprained wrist she'd incurred by being a *primadonna*.

But love really was blind, Sam had decided, because when Dallas had joshed with Pepper, asking if he'd trade the experience for a million-dollar lottery ticket, he'd said, "Nope."

Even though Pepper had gone home for the holidays, he'd get a chance to see the movie later. Inez had given it to Sam in thanks for her help with Bayfire and for Ace's surprise appearance in the movie, and Sam knew the DVD would be passed back and forth from the ranch house to the bunkhouse many times that winter.

Sam put the digging bar away and headed for the warm house.

Sausage, biscuits, and a plate of orange slices sat on the kitchen table, but the room was empty and quiet. Then she heard Dad's voice rumble from the living room.

"It's against my better judgment, I tell you, but I'm doing it!"

He didn't shout, exactly, but he'd raised his voice, and that was rare.

Sam stood still and listened. She heard feet crossing the floor upstairs, in Gram's room.

"I don't know why one of them can't do it, seein' she's set on goin'," Dad added more quietly.

"Three simple reasons," Brynna answered. "First, she doesn't trust Dallas's driving in bad weather. Second, she says Ross drives too slowly and she wants to do her turn with the therapy horse and drop off Sweetheart's winter blanket, then finish up a little Christmas shopping."

"Now, wait just a doggone minute. I never signed on for shoppin'—"

"—and third, Wyatt-Forster-love-of-my-life, you are driving me stark, staring mad and I need you out of the house for a few hours!"

"Now, B.," Dad began patiently.

"You watch every mouthful I eat and tell me to chew my food more completely so that I don't choke," Brynna began. "You check each step I take walking across a room and tell me to slow down, so that I don't fall. When I'm standing up, you ask me if I shouldn't lie down. When I do, you loom over me, watching my tummy to see if the baby squirms because you're afraid she or he won't have enough room to stretch."

Sam started giggling. She couldn't help it. Brynna was absolutely right. Gram, Brynna, and Sam had begun meeting each other's eyes each time Dad fussed.

"You got all your chores done?" Dad bawled toward the swinging door between the living room and kitchen.

"Yes, sir," Sam called back.

She sat down at the table, smiling. Her day just kept getting better and better. Her chores were finished, and if Dad and Gram were in town, there'd be no one to crack the whip. She and Brynna could relax and do whatever they wanted.

Sam just hoped Brynna had gotten all that compulsive cleaning out of her system. Yesterday when Sam had come home after the accident, Brynna had not only emptied Gram's sewing closet, she'd taken out all the odds and ends of fabric, then washed, dried, and folded them before putting them back.

Sam had snagged one piece of material that had warm memories for her, but she hadn't mentioned it to her stepmother for fear it would offend her new-found sense of order.

"Don't she just look proud as a pouter pigeon," Dad said to Sam as he came into the kitchen with Brynna. Her hand was tucked through his elbow as if they were on their way to a dance, Sam thought, but Brynna did look pretty smug.

Sam made a sound that indicated her mouth was full, even though she just really didn't want to comment on Dad's defeat.

As Gram whisked into the room carrying a big purple horse blanket she'd had specially made for Sweetheart in New Mexico, Dad started talking to Sam.

"Ross and Dallas are to stay put in case you need anything," Dad said. "I put snow chains on the truck tires and the Buick in case one or the other of 'em won't start."

"Dear," Brynna said quietly, but pointedly, "there's been a helicopter up this morning and each time one goes up it costs a thousand dollars, and—"

"'Norman White's not a man to waste money.'

Yeah, I heard that, but he's new to this country and I don't trust his weather judgment."

"I have zero symptoms—except for being as ungainly as a whale—and I have a telephone, a cell phone, the ranch radio—"

"I wound up the emergency radio, too, in case of a power failure," Dad put in.

"—a totally capable daughter, two cowboys, and a week and a half to go until my due date!" Then, before he could respond, Brynna stood on her toes, maneuvered the swell of the baby so that she could kiss Dad's cheek, and smiled as she wiggled her fingers in a wave good-bye, about an inch from his nose.

Gram slipped out the door and it looked like Dad was about to follow, but he stopped the door from closing after him to say, "Samantha, you've got that hardship driver's license. Drivin' in snow's just like driving in mud. Keep goin' slow but sure, pedal down, but not too hard—"

"Wyatt, for heaven's sake, where *do* you think Ross and Dallas'd be that Sam would have to drive to town in a snowstorm?" Gram asked, and then she must have grabbed Dad's sleeve and yanked, because he disappeared and the door slammed.

Brynna sank into the chair across the table from Sam. She listened to Dad's truck crunch over the gravel road Ross had cleared and waited as his tires thumped across the bridge. Then she waited some more, eyes closed with her head leaned against the chair back.

When her lids finally opened to show the sparkle of her blue eyes, Brynna said, "How about passing me one more biscuit and a dab of that strawberry jam?"

Chapter Sixteen

Yawning, Sam repositioned the pillow behind her head and stretched her stockinged toes until they touched the far arm of the couch. She usually preferred watching television from Dad's chair. That's where she'd started out and Brynna had picked the couch, but after they'd watched the film sent by Inez Garcia, Brynna had asked to switch places while they watched one of Sam's favorite movies, *The Little Mermaid*. Now, Sam thought, the couch suited her just fine.

Wind moaned around the corners of the ranch house and snow patted the windows, but each time Sam rose to put another log on the fire and stare outside, the snow depth looked about the same.

Brynna watched Sam watch the snow, but she didn't get up.

"If it's like this tomorrow and you want to go ride, use my cold-weather gear," Brynna told her.

"I don't know," Sam said. "I'm feeling pretty lazy."

"If you change your mind," Brynna said, picking through a bowl of cold popcorn, "it's in that little maple wood trunk in the bottom of my closet. I didn't have the figure for it this year," she said with a lopsided smile.

Sam turned away from the window. The snow must be melting as it fell. She wedged a chunky log into the fireplace. It ought to last for at least an hour.

When the movie credits rolled over the TV screen, Brynna asked Sam, "More dancing crustaceans? Or do you want to watch the Inez movie once more? I can't believe they caught the Phantom on film."

Caught the Phantom. Sam's heart responded, thudding in panic, before her brain explained the words. She must be closer to sleep than she thought.

Sam wiggled into a sitting position before she reminded Brynna, "The Phantom part won't be in the real movie."

"Who cares? *We* can watch him forever."

Brynna groaned, threw off a knitted comforter, and kneaded a muscle spasm in her leg. Each time she did stuff like that, Sam felt nervous, but she tried not to be as paranoid as Dad.

"Honey, switch places with me, will you?" Brynna asked. "Again?" she added sheepishly. With difficulty, she slid her feet into knee-high, fleece-lined shoes that were not quite boots or bedroom slippers.

"Sure," Sam said. She stood, made way for Brynna to get by, then plopped into Dad's chair.

"I don't know how I can feel restless and sleepy at the same time," Brynna said. She fidgeted on the couch, despite the pillows piled under her feet and her head. Then, with a heavy sigh, she said, "Watch whatever you . . ." The sentence ended with a ladylike snore.

Sam retrieved the comforter Brynna had discarded and pulled it up to her chin. She clicked the remote to silence the television. Through drowsy eyes, she looked across the room at the freshly laundered red flannel she'd sneaked from the reorganized sewing cabinet.

Once, it had been a nightgown, but she'd used part of it to make the first bridle the Phantom had ever worn. Back then he'd been Blackie, an ebony two-year-old, and Sam could still see the dramatic picture the stallion had made wearing the soft red halter.

If she had to tame him again, she hoped he'd remember. She could cut the cloth now and begin making a headstall, but she felt superstitious about it, almost as if fate would guarantee the Phantom's capture if she did.

Instead, Sam reached for the mystery novel she'd left on the table and began reading.

Her eyes kept closing. Too groggy to follow the clues, Sam stared at the flames in the fireplace. She kind of liked standing guard this way, especially when there was nothing to do except watch TV and read. Brynna would probably be more comfortable if she shucked off those bootie things, Sam thought, but since her stepmother was fast asleep, she left her alone.

Cougar leaped up onto Sam's lap and burrowed under the comforter. His claws kneaded her leg gently as he purred, and then he was quiet.

The first thing Sam noticed when she awoke was the cold. The log had burned down to a charred lump and she didn't hear the heater running, but there was a sunny glare of light around the curtains. *Weird,* Sam thought.

Stifling a groan as she tried to straighten knees that had been hammered and tossed around in the bus yesterday, Sam stood, then wobbled over to pull back the curtain.

Wow. Snow came down in flakes and clumps, falling as if the ranch house stood in a snow globe shaken by a crazy child.

On the couch, Brynna huffed in frustration. She must be having trouble getting comfortable.

Then Brynna sat up. She pushed back the red

frazzles of her braid and tsked her tongue.

"How did he know?"

Sam's stomach dropped so suddenly, she was sure she could have found it under the house if she'd gone looking for it.

There was no point in trying to shift the sense of Brynna's words. They could only mean one thing: Dad had been right. Today was the day Brynna would have the baby.

"Do you feel okay?" Sam noticed her hand was trembling as she released her grip on the curtain.

"Not really," Brynna confessed. She winced and locked her fingers together across her huge middle.

"I'll get your suitcase," Sam said. Sprinting up the stairs, she heard Brynna say something about calling the bunkhouse.

Good, Sam thought, *I could use some help*. Suitcase right where it was supposed to be, Sam checked it off her mental list. So was Brynna's purse with her medical information inside.

Boots . . . boots . . . there! Sam snagged her best snow boots from beside her bed and pounded back down the stairs.

In about two minutes, she'd laced on her boots extra tightly and she and Brynna were outside.

Brynna held her coat together with one hand and in the other she grasped a plastic baggie filled with tiny pink lemonade ice cubes. Gram had sworn that sucking on them during labor would give Brynna extra energy. Though Brynna had laughed at the idea before, she'd apparently decided that since the real moment was here, she'd give Gram's idea a try.

"We're ready," Brynna said, "but . . ."

Not all of their escape plan was going so well.

The truck had bogged down in the snow. Its rear wheels were spinning out. Then it jumped a rut in the ranch yard as Ross tried to drive closer to the porch.

"Stay there!" Brynna yelled into the wind, and made a "halt" motion at Ross. Then she held on to Sam's arm and began making her way across the ranch yard.

As they walked, Sam could see Ross inside the truck cab. He leaned forward to rub at the windshield fogged by his breath, and gunned the engine again. The truck spun loose from its first sticking point, but it wallowed ahead in slow motion as the bottom of the truck scraped on snow.

What had happened to the perfect path they'd shoveled? How could the storm have dumped so much snow, so fast?

The truck stuck again, and this time Sam smelled something like burning rubber.

Dallas darted behind the truck. Using the short shovel, he dug down to the gravel. *Good idea,* Sam thought as gray materialized beneath the white.

Since Dallas and Ross were doing all they could to free the truck, Sam wiped snowflakes from her eyelashes and studied Brynna.

Brynna's freckles stood out, rust-red against her pale, perspiring face. With her jaw set and eyes shut, she swayed, struggling to stay upright.

Hurry, Sam thought as she watched Dallas sprinkle something from a bag—kitty litter?—around the truck's back tires, doing everything he could to make the tires grip. The tires kept spinning, spitting gravel back at him, and Dallas threw the bag down in disgust.

He marched up to the driver's-side window and rapped on it.

"Forget it!" he shouted at Ross, then took long, stomping steps toward Gram's Buick.

"This'll work," Sam assured Brynna, but now her stepmother's face was dreamy.

Sam was prepared for Brynna to be tense and in pain, but Brynna looked as if she'd left her body for another world. It was kind of creepy.

The truck's engine went silent in mid-whine and Ross climbed out. Tugging his dark Stetson down to his nose, he didn't look over at Sam and Brynna. He followed Dallas to the Buick, swept his coat sleeve across the car's windshield, and cleared the glass of snow. For a few seconds.

Dallas dug at the snow in front of the car, clearing a path for the tires. Ross started the engine with a roar. Then he rolled down a window to motion Sam and Brynna into the backseat.

"Let's go," Sam said, and they plunged into the wind-whipped flakes, eyes set on the Buick's back door.

Sam held the door open, but Brynna glanced down at Dallas. He'd thrown the shovel aside. They could see dirt clinging to his palms and fingertips.

"He's going to give himself a heart attack," Brynna shouted. "Make him quit."

Sam didn't have to. As soon as Brynna plopped down in the backseat, Ross shouted "Get back!" and Dallas jumped away from the car.

Sam slammed the car door, crossed her fingers, and leaned forward, as if that would help the car go.

Fishtailing through the snow, the Buick headed for the bridge. Brynna covered her eyes, laughing in relief, as they shot over the wooden boards.

They reached the other side before the Buick slowed, then stuck solid.

"D-d-dang it!" Ross struck the steering wheel with the heel of his hand.

Sam looked through the back window. Through the coating of snow, she made out Dallas pushing against the back of the car. As the engine screamed, Dallas tried to rock the Buick loose.

"I can help," Sam said, unsnapping her seat belt.

"No." Brynna grabbed Sam's arm. Hard. "I'm going back inside. We can do this, Sam."

Maybe you *can,* Sam's mind wailed.

"M-ma'am," Ross protested, turning to appeal to

Brynna, but she shook her head so hard, her wet braid lashed Sam's cheek.

"Time's up," Brynna said.

Her sigh told Sam that even if the Buick came loose this instant, they weren't going to make it to the hospital before the baby came.

Brynna reached for the door handle and all but tumbled out into the snow, but she was up and standing by the time Sam rounded the back of the car.

Brynna stared upward as if the cold flakes felt good on her face, but her relieved stance didn't last. As if someone had roped her knees and jerked them forward, she gave into her labor pains, falling to her knees and leaning forward with both palms in the snow.

Before Sam could ask for help, Ross was there. He swooped Brynna up into his arms.

"I can walk," she insisted faintly, but Ross didn't notice.

As they made their way toward the house, Sam thought it had a weird glow, greenish, like Oz or like a spaceship, but it was probably just the house lights, diffused through the snowflakes. Or maybe it was stress.

Sam only knew that once they got inside and had this baby, life would never be the same.

After that, things went fast.

As Brynna settled on the couch again, Sam

started to phone the doctor, but Brynna said it would be a waste of time and money.

"Dr. Wadia is on call at the hospital tonight and I bet there's an emergency room full of people who've had snow-related accidents. We'll be fine, Sam."

Then, with her eyebrows lowered and kind of kinked in an expression Sam couldn't interpret, Brynna ordered Dallas and Ross to leave. They seemed to have expected it, but Sam hated to see them go, and it must have shown in her expression, because Dallas touched her shoulder, winked, and said, "We'll be just outside."

Brynna lay on her side on the couch. The snow had silenced every sound but the grandfather clock's swinging pendulum.

It wasn't enough to have Dallas and Ross nearby or to have a stack of books, Sam thought. Brynna had taken good care of herself during her pregnancy. Everything would probably turn out fine, but helping Dark Sunshine give birth was totally different from helping Brynna.

Suddenly, Sam knew what to do.

"I'm calling Three Ponies," Sam blurted. "Jake's mom has had six kids."

"That's a good idea, Sam," Brynna said, and though her eyes stayed closed, Sam saw the kink in her brows vanish. "I hope you can get through."

Please, please, please let the phone be working, Sam prayed as she dialed.

"Hello?"

Sam felt her neck muscles go floppy at the comforting sound of Jake's voice.

"Jake?"

"What's wrong?"

He must have heard her worry in the way she'd pronounced his name, because there was no sullen dullness in his voice. He sounded alert, on guard, and ready.

Sam almost laughed with relief. This was not the voice from the school parking lot, saying "Your friend ain't here no more." This was the voice of her friend and he was where he'd always been, standing right beside her.

"Brynna's in labor and it's just the two of us here," Sam said.

"Man oh man," Jake said quietly.

"Do you think your mom—"

"Yeah, she'll know what to do."

Sam heard Maxine Ely's voice ask a question in the background and wondered how it would feel to have a house full of people with only one "she."

"We'll be there as soon as we can," Jake said, before he explained to his mother.

"But Jake, the roads are bad. We tried to drive and—" Sam broke off at Brynna's sudden gasp.

"We'll be there," Jake repeated. "You just hang in there, Brat."

While they waited, Sam followed Brynna's instructions and called on some of the stuff she'd memorized from Gram's home-birth handbook. She joined in Brynna's deep breathing, gave her the pink lemonade ice cubes, and listened for tires crunching into the ranch yard.

Once, Sam made it as far as the big kitchen window and saw nothing but endless white before Brynna called her back and asked where the heck Wyatt was—as if she'd forgotten she'd been the one to send Dad away.

Sam rebraided Brynna's hair when the tendrils that stuck in waves to her face annoyed her.

Jake and his mom couldn't get through, Sam thought in despair. What if they'd been hurt?

She could call Dr. Scott! Sure, he was a veterinarian, but maybe he'd be in the neighborhood and he could just drop by and take over!

Sam covered her face with both hands. Was it a measure of her desperation that calling the vet sounded like such a good idea?

It had been nearly an hour since Jake had told her to hang in there. She was trying, but Brynna was getting really uncomfortable.

"Do I hear Blaze barking?" Brynna asked.

Sam held her breath to listen and all at once she heard it, too. Blaze *was* barking.

Sam ran into the kitchen and stared through the window over the sink. She saw two horses being led toward the barn. Snow clung to their manes and their dark bodies looked identical. She couldn't make out who was leading them, but if Blaze was barking—

"Sam, open up! I'm freezing!"

The knocking was muffled, but rapid. The voice was female and Sam couldn't remember locking the door.

She hadn't.

Wearing a puffy red coat that covered her from head to ankles, Mrs. Ely fell inward in a puff of snow. She stayed on her feet, despite Blaze. The Border collie bounded in beside her, skidding on wet feet as he barked in excitement.

"What do you think of this crazy weather?" Mrs. Ely asked.

"How did you—" Sam broke off, replaying the scene she'd glimpsed from the window. The only two horses she knew that looked so much alike were Witch and Chocolate Chip. "You rode over?"

"Dashing through the snow," Mrs. Ely said, nodding. "The roads are closed. Heck Ballard's out there with some guys he's deputized and they're not letting anyone through, even with four-wheel drive or chains."

"I'm so glad to see you," Sam moaned.

"Even though I'm no midwife, I guess having six babies qualifies me as something of an expert."

Dizzied by Mrs. Ely's rapid-fire words, Sam took a minute to gather her thoughts.

Scolding Blaze, Maxine shrugged off her coat and hung it on the front porch.

"So how is she? Napping?" she asked when she returned.

"No," Brynna called from the other room and Maxine hurried in to help.

Sam only wondered once what had become of Jake.

An hour passed like a minute, and then Brynna gasped, "Just about there."

Brynna's sweat-sheened face took on the look of a woman running the last minutes of a race. Then, the baby was emerging.

"You go ahead, Sam," Maxine Ely said gently.

"Go ahead and what?"

"Take him," Maxine said.

And then she was holding him.

Sam couldn't believe she held a little person slippery as a fish, but perfect in every human detail. While Maxine dabbed at the baby's nose and mouth, Sam returned the baby's gray-eyed stare. She had a brother.

"Is he breathing?" Brynna asked.

"Of course he is," Maxine cooed.

The baby answered, too. Giving a single, red-faced bleat, he shook a tiny curled fist at Sam.

"Isn't he supposed to cry?" Sam asked. "That's not really crying, is it?"

"Don't forget," Brynna said in a faded voice. "Cody's one of you stubborn Forsters."

Cody?

Maxine and Brynna were laughing, but Sam was thinking the name belonged to a calf roper or a high-desert cowboy, not a teeny little baby.

But when Maxine took Cody from Sam and laid him on Brynna's chest, Brynna kept talking to Cody as if he understood.

"Yes, he's one of you stubborn Forsters," she said again, "and he plans on doing things his own way, starting with being born at home, right here on River Bend Ranch."

Chapter Seventeen

Sam couldn't remember ever feeling so proud as she was the moment she flung open the kitchen door. Of course, Brynna had done most of the work, and Maxine had made sure everything was done correctly, but she'd stood by, helping, hadn't she? And the baby had turned out absolutely fine.

Sam gathered herself to plunge into the falling snow, headed for the bunkhouse, but she didn't get very far.

Shoulders hunched inside bulky coats, wiping their noses and stamping their boots against the cold, Ross and Dallas waited on the front porch.

"I have a little brother named Cody," Sam announced.

"Now, do ya?" Dallas said, face covered with a grin.

"That's fine, just fine." Ross nodded about ten times before reaching out to pump her arm in a handshake.

"This is so weird, but he's really cute. Do you want to see him?"

"Later," Dallas said. "Just now we're going to go make some coffee. Neither me nor Ross wanted to be the one to hike over to the bunkhouse and make it. We were afraid we might miss something. And Jake—"

"Where is Jake?" Sam asked.

"Don't know," Dallas said. "He didn't want to come inside because he was afraid you might ask him to help."

"He seemed kinda squeamish," Ross joked.

"But we're good and ready to go fire up that stove now," Dallas said, "'less you need something?"

Sam's mind spun with the names of everyone she should call, of all she should be doing for Brynna and the baby, but Brynna had only wanted a long drink of water and Maxine had brought it to her.

Sam remembered how Brynna had smiled while Cody, eyes tightly closed, nuzzled her neck and made little kissing movements with his lips.

"Samantha?" Dallas said. "They're both well, inside, aren't they? No fever or nothin'?"

Dallas's voice jerked her back and Sam shook her

head. "No, sorry. Brynna says she's fine, and Maxine thinks so, too, but I'll keep watch. I was, I don't know, drifting, I guess, but the horses . . ."

"Horses," Ross echoed, tilting his head to one side.

"Should the horses be in the barn?" Sam asked.

"Ace and your filly are in the barn, but the rest of 'em are in the run-in shed, cozied up and happy. We'll give 'em some extra hay, though," Dallas said.

"That's good," Sam said, but she was thinking of Dad. "I wish I could call my dad."

"Jake said he heard Sheriff Ballard was holding traffic outside Alkali," Dallas told her.

Which meant there was no way to reach him, Sam thought. But then Ross and Dallas were nodding and touching the brims of their frosty hats in good-bye.

By the time they were halfway across the ranch yard, both men were covered in white. Dallas looked like a bowlegged snowman. Ross lumbered like a polar bear. Both of them were chuckling as Sam closed the door and went to take another look at her new baby brother.

Inside, Sam turned the heater up. Thank goodness the storm hadn't brought a power failure, she thought as she hurried to the phone.

Hand on the receiver, she glanced at the clock. It was just after three. The horse therapy program would have ended. She was surprised Dad and Gram hadn't called from someplace in town. Cell phone service was too spotty to depend upon, so Dad wouldn't carry one, and the radios they'd had installed in the ranch vehicles wouldn't work that far away.

They were probably someplace on the road between Darton and home, Sam told herself, unless they were shopping. If so, that wouldn't last long. Dad would nag Gram to rush and they'd probably be back in the truck half an hour after they'd found a parking place.

Who should she call first? Jen? Aunt Sue in San Francisco? Everyone at Deerpath Ranch?

As she thought of Deerpath Ranch and the Dream Catcher program, Sam pictured shivering but determined Darby Carter.

That kid was something else, Sam thought. Though she was shy, sickly, and more comfortable with books than with people, she had guts and loved horses. She definitely had the makings of a cowgirl. Sam would bet Darby was helping with the golden mustang and the orphan foals right now, with her inhaler in one pocket and her book in the other.

Smiling, Sam picked up the phone. There was a dial tone, sort of, but a weird scratchy sound was in the background. She dialed Jen's number and the scratchy sound got louder, but nothing else happened. She checked to make sure the phone was plugged into the wall, and it was. She hung up, picked up, and this time there wasn't even a dial tone.

How lucky was she that it had been working when she called Three Ponies? Sam gave a loud sigh, then peeked into the living room. Brynna and Cody were asleep on the couch and Maxine was dozing in Dad's recliner, so Sam decided to make herself some lunch. After all, it had been a long time since breakfast.

When Sam settled down with a bowl of soup, she crunched crackers over the top. It was a habit Gram called rude, but she figured she deserved a reward. Sam was finishing off her last bite when Brynna awakened hungry and Maxine helped Sam feed the new mother everything she wanted, so she'd be strong enough to feed Cody everything *he* wanted.

Finally, Sam washed dishes as she wondered what had become of Jake. He'd ridden over with his mom, and he'd slipped inside once. Though she had been upstairs, Sam had heard him tell Maxine he'd gotten through to his dad on their walkie-talkies, and let him know they'd be spending the night at River Bend Ranch, but then he'd disappeared outside again.

Now, Sam heard Jake stamping snow off his boots. The outside door opened and closed. It had to be Jake, because Dallas or Ross would have knocked. Sam heard a rustling sound and guessed he was hanging his coat on the porch alongside his mother's, and leaving his hat there, too, but she didn't turn away from the sink until she heard him say,

"Dark as the inside of a cow out there."

"Thanks for helping," Sam said. She wiped her hands dry on her jeans as she turned around.

Jake's blue corduroy shirt looked surprisingly neat, but his hair hung wet on his shoulders and damp spots were spreading.

"Thanks for riding over here with your mom, too."

Jake shrugged and glanced toward the living room.

Sam answered Jake's unasked question. "They're talking about baby stuff."

"I saw him. Cody." Jake seemed to turn the name over and find it to his liking. "He's sure little." Jake rubbed the back of his neck and looked longingly at the door.

Even though they both felt awkward and nothing had been settled between them, Sam didn't want Jake to leave.

She'd give him *one* chance to act civilized and just go on as friends.

"Do you want something to eat?" Sam asked. "I could make a sandwich that probably wouldn't poison you."

"Sure," Jake said, then he stood right behind her, staring over her shoulder as she sliced bread, spread it with mustard, then layered on roast beef and cheese. He didn't give her directions or advice, and Sam decided she liked him watching and accepting a lot better than if Jake had sat down at the table, assuming he'd be waited upon.

Gram would have slapped his hand if she'd seen him snatch the sandwich from the cutting board and take a bite before Sam gave him a plate, but she just asked, "Do you want something to drink?"

Jake stopped chewing to ask, "Tea?"

That was a surprise, but Sam filled the tea kettle and set it to boil. She stood there and stared at it.

While Jake ate in silence, Sam thought back to the day he'd gotten mad. She still couldn't figure out why. She could only come up with jealousy, but Jake couldn't be dumb enough to think she had a crush on Kit, just because she'd interviewed him.

No, it made more sense that because Kit had arrived home to everyone's open arms and admiration and then kept calling Jake Baby Bear as if he were a little kid, not a hard-working rancher, Jake was irritated with the rest of his family. Maybe he'd just felt it was easier to yell at her than at his entire family.

The tea kettle's shriek startled them both, and Maxine bolted through the swinging door.

"Sorry," Sam apologized.

"She's awake. We're talking about diapers," Maxine said. "I just wanted to ask if you could make a cup for me."

"Sure," Sam said, but Maxine had already vanished back into the other room.

"Diapers," Jake said, shuddering.

Sam dipped a tea bag in a cup of hot water. She watched it float up and sink down, feeling half hypnotized when Jake said, "Kit *was* lying to you."

Sam waited for him to go on. She didn't have the energy to fight, but since Jake rarely felt like talking, she would listen.

"Quinn heard Kit talking to my parents and told me while we were out in the barn, that day you were over. Kit's not going back to bronc riding. All that stuff about being back in the chutes with his buddy Pani?"

Sam nodded, remembering.

"He can't."

"Why?" Sam asked.

"He fell with a bronc. It rolled on his wrist. Not his free hand. His rope hand."

It took Sam a second to picture a rodeo rider holding single-handedly to a rope rein while his other hand waved in the air as the contest required.

"It crushed eight bones to dust." Jake brushed his fingers over the back of his hand and up to his shirt cuff.

"And *that* made you mad?" Sam couldn't believe he hadn't felt sorry for his brother.

"I know," Jake said. He made a calming motion. "And I do feel bad, but I just went off on this mental tangent."

Jake held his head with both hands and his look of confusion made Sam laugh.

"But you're awful for being mad at him, and me," she said.

"Okay, I'm awful," Jake admitted, but he sounded as if he were about to make a second confession. "Here's the thing. I wasn't really jealous of you and Kit. I wanted to be, kind of, but that wasn't it at all. It was worse than that."

"Okay," Sam said, carefully.

"Kit's either fooling himself or lying to the rest of us about going back to rodeo. And when I leave for college, he'll take over Three Ponies."

"Can he even ride?" Sam asked.

"For normal purposes, I think he could ride even if he'd lost his whole arm," Jake said, and Sam winced. "He's so good on a horse." Jake sounded envious. "He didn't lie about that. When I was little I remember Mom saying Kit was ambidextrous. I thought it had to do with ambushes, 'til she explained it meant he could use both hands to do things.

"But of all of us, I'm the one . . ." Jake blew out a loud breath. "I'm the one of us kids who's cared most about the ranch. If I leave it to him for four years, there'll be no getting it back."

And that *would* be worse than her having a crush on Kit, Sam agreed. But then her mind shifted to a picture of Jake with his hair long like it used to be, setting off for Great Basin College with Witch in a trailer and Singer sitting on the truck bench beside him. His future would be waiting at the end of the road ahead, and he shouldn't have to worry about losing his position at Three Ponies to Kit.

"But wait, is that what Kit wants to do?" Sam asked. "Stay home and run the family ranch?"

"Why wouldn't he?" Jake asked.

"So you haven't asked him," Sam pointed out.

Jake shook his head and lifted his cup. His hands dwarfed Gram's china tea cup.

"I forgot to take your mom her tea!" Sam said. "I'll be right back."

It took her a few extra minutes, because Maxine asked her to bring Brynna her maps and a pencil from upstairs. Maxine rolled her eyes and Sam couldn't believe it, either. Brynna had been working with her BLM maps for two months. Surely she could forget about them today.

When she returned, Jake's jaw was set hard, but he didn't look mad. His eyes tested hers with a look that was almost . . . timid?

"What?" Sam demanded. Jake must have done something terrible to be scared of *her*.

"There's something else," he said.

"Spit it out," Sam told him.

Jake blew his cheeks full of air and looked at her sideways.

"Look . . ." Sam heard her voice, loud as a gunshot. She lowered it to a whisper. "I helped deliver a baby today, Jake Ely. Do you really think anything you're about to say will shock me?"

Jake shuddered as he had when his mother mentioned diapers.

"It's not shockin', exactly. And it's not like you haven't thought of it, but, what I mean to say is this. I'm sorry."

Sam sighed. Jake was an idiot for making such a big deal out of an apology, but he probably didn't do it very often.

"So, we're friends again?" Sam asked, trying to sound casual.

"Oh, yeah," he said, pushing his black hair away from his mustang eyes.

And Sam was really glad.

Chapter Eighteen

At the same time, both Sam and Jake heard water dripping outside. Jake walked to the door, opened it, and stood staring out for a minute. Sam was about to order him to close the door because he was letting out all the kitchen warmth, but she didn't want to sound like Gram.

"Snow melting off the roofs. It's thawing already," he said. "Better hope it doesn't freeze up overnight, or it'll be darn icy and they still won't open the roads."

Sam was eager to have Dad home. He didn't even know about Cody yet. He must be going crazy, wanting to call.

Sam heard one horse neigh—she thought it was Strawberry—and another snort. They probably welcomed the warming temperatures.

When Jake closed the door, he looked thoughtful. Sam would bet he was still thinking about Kit and Three Ponies.

"'Course Dad told Mom that Kit's mulling over an offer to be head wrangler on his friend Pani's ranch."

"And your dad told you?" Sam asked.

"Well, no. Nate was puttin' a blade on the front of the tractor to use as a snowplow, and—"

"Your dad didn't see him while he was telling your mom?" Sam guessed. She shook her head. "And I bet you guys would say *girls* gossip."

Jake helped Sam carry the baby's cradle downstairs. It was bigger and heavier than it looked, and tough to manage when you were the one walking backward down the steps, but Brynna had said the stairs up to her bedroom looked insurmountable.

It wasn't until Maxine said she didn't mind sleeping in Dad's big chair and Jake said he was headed out to the bunkhouse that Sam knew for sure that the Elys were spending the night. It was a weird sort of slumber party, but Sam was glad they were staying. What Jake, Dallas, or Ross couldn't handle, Maxine probably could.

Sam had turned off all the kitchen lights, but left on the one on the porch when the telephone rang.

"Got it!" she shouted, then grabbed it quick before it could stop functioning. "Hello?"

"Sam, at last! Honey, we almost made it home.

They've got the road closed at Alkali. At least we're in out of the truck and Clara says she's willing to stay open all night for the six customers who're stuck here."

"Dad! You were right—" Sam began.

"No," Dad cut her off, but then there was a moment of silence before he whispered, "She didn't."

"His name is Cody," Sam said. "But you probably knew that."

"We're—we *were* still discussin' it. Guess 'Karen' was out of the question, huh?"

Then Dad let go with a cowboy yell that almost deafened Sam. She heard a muddle of voices, one of them Gram's, and Dad announcing he had a son, before she realized Brynna was standing beside her.

Brynna's hair was wound up in a messy topknot with a pencil stuck through it. She wore a gray sweat-shirt that might be Dad's and she looked more alert than she had since breakfast. She waved a hand in front of Sam's eyes as if breaking a trance.

"Oh! I should have waited and let you tell him," Sam said. "But it just slipped out."

"I'm glad it was you," Brynna said, patting Sam's arm.

"B?" Dad yelled as Sam handed Brynna the phone.

Sam eased out of the room so her parents could talk, and she realized she really did feel like Brynna was hers.

"This is working out just fine, isn't it?" Maxine

asked as Sam entered the living room.

"Yeah," Sam agreed.

She stared down at Cody. Brynna had dressed him in a fuzzy yellow sleeper and Sam pictured him walking someday, following her around like a baby duck.

Weariness and contentment enfolded Sam. She plucked Cougar off the couch from the warm spot Brynna had temporarily abandoned, and held him against her shoulder.

"I think we'll sleep in tomorrow morning," Sam whispered to the purring cat.

"Sam?" Brynna's voice carried to her.

Sam stiffened. Brynna didn't sound happy.

Cougar struggled to jump from Sam's arms. She let him, then hurried past Maxine, who watched her with raised eyebrows.

"Your dad wants to tell you something," Brynna said, but she didn't leave. She held on to one of the kitchen chairs as she waited.

"Dad?" Sam asked.

"First, I need your promise you won't go anywhere tonight, no matter what."

"What's wrong?" Sam demanded.

"Swear to me, Sam," Dad insisted, "or you'll just have to wait until I get home. Tomorrow."

That's not fair, Sam thought. How could she make a promise based on nothing but Dad saying she had no choice?

"I can't—?"

"Brynna said you were amazin' today, better than anyone else, includin' me, could've been."

Sam glanced over at Brynna. She was sketching something on the back of an envelope she'd pulled from the bill box on Gram's hutch. "Now, make me even prouder, honey, and say you'll be sensible," Dad finished.

"Okay," Sam said, but she didn't like it.

"Your buckskin is gone," Dad said.

Of course Dark Sunshine was gone. Had Brynna gotten confused and told Dad that? During this mixed-up day, could she, and Dad, too, have forgotten the mare had been taken to the pasture by Clara's coffee shop during weaning?

But wait. Dad said he was in Alkali, at Clara's. Sam drew in a deep breath and let it out with shuddering slowness.

Gone could mean more than *vanished*. It could mean Dark Sunshine was dead.

"Gone?" Sam asked, finally.

"In the middle of that snowstorm, a truck driver making a delivery at Clara's was backing up—"

Sam pulled her arms closer to herself, fighting the chill of despair. Poor Tempest. Poor Sunny.

"And he bumped into a fence post," Dad went on. "Probably didn't even know he'd done it and neither would we, but when Teddy Bear showed up at Clara's front door, we went back there to see what had happened and saw the tire tracks.

"Sure enough, two sections of fence were sagging almost to the ground. It's a wonder all the horses didn't follow her."

"She got out, you mean?" Sam asked, afraid to hope she had it right. "She escaped?"

"Sure." Dad's sigh said just what Sam was thinking. Dark Sunshine had never settled in like Ace or Popcorn or other captive mustangs. "She saw her chance and took it."

And then Dad's warning not to leave the ranch made sense.

Dark Sunshine wasn't dead, but where *was* she on this dark December night?

She's fine, Sam scolded herself, remembering Strawberry, just an hour ago, snorting as if it were spring.

"I won't go anywhere, Dad," Sam promised. "Even Jake can't track in the dark."

"But he *can* track in the snow. For him, it should be like followin' a roadmap. That's why—if everything's as it should be in the morning—you can set out at first light."

"Thank you," Sam said, kind of surprised.

Then, for the first time in a few minutes, her eyes wandered to Brynna. She was on the verge of sleeping standing up, again, like a horse. That couldn't be safe.

"In my mind," Dad went on, "if the snow's as wet as I'm afraid it will be, you'll want to take a bigger horse than Ace—Jeep, maybe, or even Tank—but that's your call."

"Thanks, Dad," Sam said again.

"Ninety percent of the time, you've got a good level head on your shoulders," Dad said. "But we both know what happens when you're around that stallion."

What did the Phantom have to do with anything? Sam wondered as she kept her eyes clamped on Brynna.

"Now, Norman White may be a sorry excuse for a human being," Dad went on, "but—"

"Dad?" Sam interrupted. "Brynna's fallen asleep standing up again. And she's kind of slumped over a kitchen chair."

"Don't let her fall," Dad said. "But you better not be fibbin' to me, young lady, just because I'm sayin' something you don't want to hear."

"Not a chance," Sam said, and as soon as she hung up the phone, she walked Brynna back to her baby and her comforter on the couch bed.

Sam had set her alarm, afraid she'd oversleep after her full day, but she came instantly awake when she remembered Dark Sunshine was out running wild.

Sam wasn't taking any chances that she'd get cold and have to head for home. Last night she'd sorted through Brynna's trunk of winter gear and come up with riding tights, a little hood thing she thought was called a balaclava that would fit under her brown

Stetson and cover her from her chin down into her shirt, and a great insulated jacket with Velcro wrists that would close down tight over her gloves.

Jake would have all the cold weather gear he needed, since he and his mom had ridden over here at the height of the storm. That's why she hadn't warned him about today's search.

Sam tiptoed downstairs, thinking that if she just sprung the idea on Jake this morning, he wouldn't have time to make up an excuse.

Not that she'd take no for an answer. With Jake or without him, she was riding after Dark Sunshine and she wouldn't come home until she had her horse.

Everyone downstairs was still sleeping, but Sam heard the horses nosing their buckets outside, and since it wasn't late, the noise meant the horses had spotted someone moving around and hoped they'd get fed.

Sam hadn't forgotten her chores, and her gloves were too thick to cross her fingers for luck, but she was hoping she could talk Dallas and Ross into volunteering to do them, so that she and Jake could get an early start.

Jake spotted her from the barn door. Judging from the hay stuck to his clothes, he'd been feeding Ace, Tempest, Chocolate Chip, and Witch, but he paused when he saw how she was dressed.

Sam tried not to look nervous. She took long, confident strides, and tried not to think about how much she was taking for granted.

"Mornin'," Jake said, bumping his Stetson up so he could see her better.

In one breathless rush, she spilled out everything she knew about Dark Sunshine's escape.

"So, will you help me?" she asked when she'd finished.

"Can't think of anything I'd rather do, 'cept kiss a polecat," Jake said with his most annoying drawl. And then he turned and walked back into the barn.

"A polecat's a skunk, right?" Sam called after him.

Jake didn't answer. All she heard was the chiming of his spurs and the short whistle he used to call Witch.

Two hours later, Jake had picked up Dark Sunshine's trail.

Following Dad's advice, Sam had ridden Jeepers-Creepers. Dallas thought the rangy Appaloosa was the best choice because he was fit enough to break trails through the snow and conditioned enough to be out all day.

Sam wasn't sure the same went for her. She shifted, trying to get settled, as she followed Jake on Witch. Her saddle had been too small for Jeep, so she was using whatever Dallas had cinched on the horse. She didn't ask who it belonged to, because she was in a rush, and even adjusting the stirrups seemed to take forever.

They'd passed through all kinds of snow, from sticky stuff that clung to the horses' legs to a wind-sculpted blue sea frozen in the shadow of black plateaus. The footing was surprisingly good. It was so good that her mind was wandering and she was thinking about what she'd read—that countries in the far north had dozens of names for snow—when she heard a faraway throbbing sound.

Jeep must have heard it, too, or he'd picked up her awareness, because his gait changed from an easy jog to a stiff-legged trot.

"Is that thunder?" Sam asked.

"Or hooves, or helicopters," Jake muttered, reading the wide-spaced hoofprints in the snow. "Whatever it is has got your buckskin runnin' scared."

She and Jake had just been here, Sam realized. This was where she'd found Singer, and though she hadn't breathed a word of her stallion's secret to Jake, he knew as well as she that Sunny was headed back to the Phantom's hidden valley.

"There she is!" Sam said.

Sunny broke from the cover of a tall stand of sagebrush. Though she was silent, she was no more than a quarter-mile away, and both Jeep and Witch shied at her sudden appearance. Sam spotted the herd of running horses that the mare was chasing.

For a second, Dark Sunshine looked bony and dejected, and Sam ached to return her to her foal. But then the mare saw the Phantom, trailing his herd, trotting in a distracted manner as he looked back over his shoulder at the mare and the riders behind her.

As soon as she sighted the stallion, Dark Sunshine no longer looked small. She seemed to grow with each stride that took her closer to him.

Buckskin shoulders gleaming with sweat, black mane tangling in the wind, she threw her head high, flaring her nostrils to suck in the scents of wild places.

She slowed long enough to neigh.

Take me home, she called to the stallion, and he swerved away as his herd galloped on without him.

Did the Phantom recognize Dark Sunshine? Sam remembered the times the stallion had appeared on the ridge trail that overlooked River Bend's barn.

He must remember, because he hesitated, then sidestepped, tossing his mane and snorting. Silver in the morning sun, surrounded by sagebrush and snow, the stallion thundered toward the little mare.

"Sunny!" Sam shouted. "Come back, girl!"

Sunny glanced back at the sound of Sam's voice, and for a minute it looked like she might obey. But Sam was wrong.

One glance was all it took to launch the mare into a headlong run to meet the stallion.

She's running away from me, Sam realized.

Sunny had never stopped longing for the range. She'd never felt the pull to return to shelter, steady food, and human companionship. She'd only stayed as long as Tempest needed her.

Now, without the filly to hold her, the buckskin mare chose freedom.

"She's branded," Jake shouted to Sam. "You can't let her go!"

The BLM would just round her up again and charge the Forsters a trespass fee. With Norman White in charge, it was a sure thing.

Sam leaned forward in the saddle and clapped her heels to the Appaloosa's sides. Jeep leaped after the buckskin, understanding his job.

Minutes later, they had to slow down. The snow had deepened around them, and though they picked their way up the plateau at what was still a risky speed, Dark Sunshine kept drawing ahead.

Once, Jake stood in his stirrups. Was he judging the distance to the mare, deciding whether his rope would reach her?

Although she'd outdistanced Witch and Jeep, Sunny was falling behind the taller mustangs. Still, she refused to give up. Clots of foam flew from her open mouth. She lengthened her body and reached with her legs until her belly skimmed the snow.

They were almost to the mouth of the tunnel when Sam shouted, "We can't do this!"

At first she thought she heard Jake's answer.

But the echo between the treeless mountain face and the rock entrance couldn't have distorted Jake's voice into such a mighty vibration.

When the sound changed from resonance into a *whup-whup-whup* that vibrated Sam's insides, the horses were terrified, but Sam was a little relieved. At least she recognized that sound. For a moment, she'd been afraid it was something even worse.

The helicopter's rotors whipped snow into a blizzard, blinding the horses, leaving them at the mercy of a pulsating sound that stalked them like a living thing.

The chopper bobbed up from the other side of the ridge. How could it make the boulders shudder and shake? Could they really be loosening and bounding down the mountainside?

The cornice! Sam stared up to see a fracture run from the frozen wave of snow to a lone tree, and then to a rock. Gradually the crack widened.

The Phantom screamed. Jostling and shoving, he shoved the stragglers on. His teeth clacked as he forced his herd to run faster. Sam knew the stallion would draw blood and stir panic if he had to, but she didn't see him.

She couldn't take her eyes from the slab of snow sheering off and sliding her way.

Jeep reared. Jake shouted at Sam. He leaned out of his saddle, and his gloved fingers spread wide, reaching for her, for a rein, for anything to make her safe.

Black amid the torrents of white, Witch swerved,

trying to keep Jake balanced. The mare bent almost double, fighting to keep the saddle beneath him.

It was the last Sam saw of Witch and Jake, because the sky was falling and so was she.

The warm leather saddle and frantic Appaloosa peeled away from her.

She collided with slick rock, then slid within inches of the last mares' hooves as they streamed into the tunnel. She stopped with half her body inside, then pushed up on her palms, determined to crawl if she had to.

But a sound behind her rang above the tumult of snow.

The Phantom reared, silver power against the white fury of snow. When he returned to the ground, Sam flattened herself against the wall of the tunnel, praying his hooves would miss her, praying the ledge over the tunnel's mouth would break the teeth of the avalanche and protect them both.

The stallion stormed past her and Sam staggered to her feet. Hunched over and veering from side to side on unsteady legs, she ran after the stallion, in case the snow could somehow follow.

At last, the cacophony of rock and ice ended. A few final boulders shook the floor beneath her. One more, and then nothing.

She was alone in the tunnel. She'd almost reached the valley when she dared to look back.

The white glare was gone. All sound was blotted

out by the ringing in her ears.

She was sealed into the tunnel by a thousand tons of snow.

Sam walked toward the hidden home of the wild horses. She was one of them now.

Chapter Nineteen

The valley's rock walls looked safe and solid and the stream ran quietly through sparse winter grass. Everything seemed peaceful, but the mustangs weren't taking any chances.

Blacks and bays, sorrels and roans crowded together at one end of the valley, ears pricked and alert as the last few boulders bounded down the mountain outside.

As Sam thought of the moments she'd stared up into the white death of the avalanche, unable to move, she decided the horses had been a lot smarter than she had. They hadn't tried to make sense of the onslaught of snow. They hadn't watched danger rush right into them and knock them on their bellies. The mustangs, with legs flying and tails streaming, had headed for safety.

Even the foals had known to run first and think it over later, like they were now. They were a lot better suited for survival than she was.

Sam watched the horses until they decided the threat had passed. Then they drifted from the safety of their bunch. Some lined up along the stream to drink. Some ate the chilled grass and others sniffed at Dark Sunshine. But there were no squeals or nips to put the newcomer in her place.

A sense of peace settled over the valley. The horses were safe and they knew it. Only the Phantom was restless. He wandered among his mares and foals as if counting them.

The herd did seem smaller than usual, Sam thought. She didn't see the two blood bays that were always together. And what about the roan filly she called Sugar? She seemed to be missing, too.

Sam hadn't seen a single horse fall in the avalanche. Could they have been swept up into a BLM gather? Norman White had sworn the mustangs he'd captured hadn't been members of the Phantom's herd, but would he really know? If a few mustangs had wandered from their home band, Norman might have corralled them, thinking they were a separate herd.

Sam walked close to the stream once the horses had finished. She kneeled and drank.

Looking at her ragged reflection, Sam pushed the balaclava off. It had kept her warm, but it felt good to be free of the tight hood. She shook her head. Her auburn hair fell in ripples to her shoulders, as damp as if she'd just washed it.

Moisture from the snow had soaked through the hood and she wondered what had become of her old brown Stetson.

"I loved that hat," Sam muttered to herself. Then, wiping her lips with the back of her hand, Sam stood up on shaky legs.

A snort made her jump, and she turned to see the Phantom standing about five feet away. Majestic and muscled, he watched her without blinking. If she didn't know better, she'd think his gaze accused her of something, and suddenly Sam knew what it was.

She had to leave.

She wanted to sit down and nap, but she couldn't.

She had to leave the valley before Jake decided she was trapped and told everyone in the county she needed help. He'd hate telling her secret, but he'd want her rescued no matter what it cost the Phantom. She knew Jake well enough to be certain of that.

Ranchers, Sheriff Ballard, volunteer firefighters, and others would follow Jake back here. They'd bring shovels, bulldozers, maybe even dynamite. The horses' haven would not only be discovered; it would be ruined.

Hurry, Sam told herself. She had to find a way out.

The horses always came and went through the tunnel, and it was sealed with snow and boulders, maybe for good. The snow would melt in the spring, but the boulders wouldn't. Still, sky showed overhead. There had to be a path to the top edge of the valley.

Sam flexed her fingers as she looked at the steep rock walls. From here, they looked slick and smooth, but there had to be rocks she could use as handholds, and places where she could wedge her feet to climb.

Maybe she could escape in a way that the horses couldn't.

Do it now, Sam urged herself. *Before it's too late.*

The Phantom walked alongside her as she made a quick circuit of the valley, surveying the sheer cliffs. At last she saw a place to start. Even if Jake had already ridden for help, she'd get to the top and start walking along the road. When they saw her, the search party would turn back and leave the horses alone.

The stallion stopped when she did, watching as Sam looked straight up, the back of her head folding her collar, from the base of the bumpiest cliff.

"I don't know much about rock climbing," she told the horse.

She could fall. Just like before, she could hurl through emptiness until her body slammed against the ground. Only this time she'd be falling from a mile-high rock wall, not Blackie's back.

But she had no choice . . .

The Phantom shied off, running back to his herd at the sound of more snow skidding down the mountainside.

Of course, I've got a choice, Sam thought.

She could stand right here and wait to be rescued, endangering the horses she loved because she was a coward.

"Or I can just not fall," she muttered.

Sam took a shuddering breath, wishing for some sign that she was doing the right thing. She'd welcome a hawk floating in that pale blue sky, or a sun dog—one of those rainbows around the sun. She wouldn't turn down even a blue jay's squawk, but there was nothing except her own determination to start her climbing.

"Too bad," she muttered, but then she heard the Phantom coming back to her.

She filled her eyes with him, in case she never saw him again.

Sunlight sparkled on the his pale coat and fired his mane and tail with a sterling luster. Staring through his rumpled forelock, the stallion gave a low nicker. As clearly as if he'd spoken, he told her goodbye.

"You are the most wonderful horse in the world, and I love you," Sam whispered.

The stallion pawed the ground. He lowered his

kingly head, then snaked his muzzle, face, ears, and neck under her arm. Then he flipped his head, ordering her to mount up.

"I wish I could." Sam's regret didn't scare the stallion away. He leaned against her, lending her his warmth, but no matter how close he stood, the Phantom couldn't know how torn Sam was.

There was only one thing in the world she wanted more than a last ride on the Phantom. His safety.

She ignored the selfish voice in her mind that told her that one last ride would only take a few minutes.

It would also only take a few minutes for a well-meaning rescuer to blast through the tunnel, putting her horse, his herd, and their haven in danger.

Softly, Sam draped her arms around the stallion's neck.

"I can't," she whispered. "I have to go." Sam's tears wet the stallion's neck. "I didn't know, boy, that day we found Singer, but I couldn't have loved it more if I *had* known it was the last time."

Sam gave herself one more moment surrounded by the Phantom. She saw and touched nothing but the silver stallion. Then she gave him one more hug and stepped back.

He lowered his head until his forelock brushed the ground and Sam turned away to start climbing. She moved as fast as she could, gulping mountain air to fuel each scaling step, and she only looked back once.

When she did, she couldn't see the Phantom, but

her twinge of regret only lasted a second.

There, right there, was Dark Sunshine. The small mare rolled in the winter grass, kicking black legs that shaded into buckskin gold, looking happier than Sam had ever seen her before.

Even though she'd miss her, Sam knew the mare was meant to be free.

Sam had never paid much attention to her fingernails, but thirty minutes later, she'd learned she could really focus on them when they were the only thing holding her to a rock wall. Bleeding and packed with grit, they hung on until she reached a shallow shelf where she could finally put both feet down next to each other.

She was almost to the top, but the muscles in her arms trembled like jello. Could she make it without a rest?

Not only were her muscles strained and quivering, she was panting. And shivering. Sam tried not to think how much colder it was getting, the higher she climbed. At least the sun had been on this side of the valley. The snow had melted off, and though the rock was wet, it wasn't icy. She stamped her feet, hoping improved circulation would help her climb the final vertical slab.

A shower of gravel spit down on her head. She cringed away from it, then looked up, right into Jake's face.

"Didn't mean to scare you," he said at her gasp.

"How long have you been there?" Sam asked.

"A while," he said. "I didn't want to break your concentration."

Why did she suddenly feel an irresistible urge to look down, to see how far she'd climbed? The temptation was too much for her. Before her chin grazed her shoulder though, Jake sucked in a breath.

"I wouldn't do that," he said. "Take this, instead."

Jake lowered his rope to her.

She was really losing it, Sam thought. The sight of Jake's rope was as comforting as a light in the window, leading her home.

"You know how to tie a bowline knot," he said.

It wasn't a question. Sam *did* know. She just couldn't remember. Maybe it was a lack of oxygen that made her think it was better to brush off Jake's offer than admit she'd forgotten.

"I'm not going to fall. I've made it this far without the rope, and I can finish on my own," Sam said.

"No—"

"Yes," Sam insisted.

"Well, I'm kinda scared. I've *been* kinda scared. Just do it for me, will ya?"

Heartbeats couldn't drown out every other sound on earth, could they? If Jake was scared, there was a good reason she should be, too.

"Okay," Sam said, catching the end of the rope.

"It'll give me something to do if you let me talk

you through it," he said. "Now, put the end around your waist. Then take the loose end in your right hand and lay it over the top of the rope that's coming back up to me."

Suddenly, the motion felt familiar.

"Oh, yeah," Sam said. "Then I kind of flip that into a loop and—I know! This next part is where you pretend the end of the rope is a rabbit going around the tree and over the hole. . . ."

"Up outta the hole, Sam," Jake cautioned.

"I'm being careful," she assured him. "I won't dash my brains out on the rocks below."

She jerked the knot tight and looked up for Jake's approval, but he didn't waste any time saying "atta girl."

Jake's hands gripped the rope. His sleeves were pushed up and his forearms looked strong.

He wasn't going to go jump on Witch and let the Quarter Horse pull her up and over the ledge.

The two of them were doing this alone.

"Ready," she told Jake through chattering teeth, and then it was easy. He pulled as she edged her way up to the rim. With a final lurch, she was over the top, facedown on blessedly flat ground.

As soon as she'd stopped hyperventilating, Jake urged her to stand up. Then he herded her away from the edge, toward Witch.

Sam took a few steps, then stopped.

"Did you see my hat?" she asked.

"Yeah. It's buried under about a thousand tons of snow," Jake said. "I was just glad your head wasn't in it." When Sam recoiled, he added, "Maybe you'll get a new one for Christmas."

Sam nodded, walked a few more steps, then stopped again.

"Is Jeep okay?" Sam asked suddenly.

"Fine," Jake said.

"Really?" Sam asked.

"Really. No scuffs, no bruises. He just took off for home."

"Okay," Sam said, but Jake sounded a little strange.

"Don't worry none about givin' *me* heart failure," he went on. "Just fret over that rattailed Appaloosa."

"It's not like I planned this," Sam said, but Jake held up a hand for her to halt.

Sam nodded. She felt a little light-headed. It would be a good idea to save her breath until they reached Witch.

When they did, Jake swooped the mare's reins up off the ground and asked, "You gonna be like this for the rest of your life?"

"Like what?" Sam asked, watching Jake shrug on the jacket he'd left hanging on his saddle horn.

He swung into Witch's saddle, kicked his boot free of the stirrup, and offered his hand to help Sam up.

"Guess that answers my question."

Far from looking angry, Jake wore a lopsided

smile that struck Sam as hilarious. A shout of laughter burst out of her, and it was followed by unstoppable giggles. When she realized she was laughing alone, everything seemed even funnier.

Finally, Sam caught her breath enough to talk. Hands on hips, she said, "You wouldn't like me any other way."

"Put your boot in the stirrup and swing on up behind me."

"Admit it," Sam said.

"Samantha, just get on the horse."

She did, but as she locked her arms around Jake's middle and pressed her cheek against his jacket, Sam was still laughing.

The kitchen table at River Bend Ranch was crowded with pecan pies when Sam walked in. And they had company.

For some reason, she hadn't noticed Mrs. Allen's truck, if it was parked outside. She'd hugged Dad and felt him looking over her head, meeting Jake's eyes in one of those man-to-man looks that meant they'd be talking about her after she left the barn.

She'd hugged Tempest, too, but the filly had switched her tail in boredom as Sam told the filly her mother was gone.

Finally, Tempest stamped her hoof, narrowly missing Sam's boot toe, and squirmed loose to go annoy Ace.

Now Sam stood in the warm kitchen.

"Sam, are you all right?" Brynna asked, wide-eyed.

"Sure," Sam said, running her hands over her hair and brushing at the brown mud that was smeared all over her shirt. "I didn't mean to interrupt."

"That's all right," Gram said slowly, and Sam could feel her grandmother's eyes follow her as she moved into the living room.

Cody slept under a soft blue blanket. Watching his peaceful breathing, Sam finally allowed weariness to overtake her. Instead of running up to her room and changing clothes, Sam returned to the kitchen, slid into her chair, and leaned back. If she put her hands on the table, she'd collapse on her face and fall asleep.

In fact, her vision had turned blurry when Mrs. Allen reached over to pat her arm and Sam jerked alert.

"I was just telling Grace and Brynna what a plucky little heroine you were on Saturday," Mrs. Allen said.

Sam shook her head. She wasn't sure what *plucky* meant, but she'd bet that bookworm Darby would. Still, she knew she hadn't done anything heroic.

Stretching out in the snow to comfort a stricken horse—now *that* was heroic.

"How's Darby?" Sam asked.

"Amazing," Mrs. Allen said flatly. "She won't

leave that sorrel filly unless it's to help bottle-feed the orphan foals. She wouldn't even sleep inside the house until I threatened to call her mother."

"Where have I heard of behavior like that before?" Brynna asked slyly.

"Trudy just stopped by to pick up her Christmas pie," Gram said.

"And to look at your darling brother," Mrs. Allen said.

"And we were talking about having a New Year's Eve bonfire. Remember, the last one we had was such fun. . . ."

Despite her efforts to keep her eyelids wide, Sam dozed off. At least, she was pretty sure she had, because the next thing she heard was the sound of a low-flying helicopter.

"I've had enough of those things!" Mrs. Allen snarled.

Gram and Brynna were agreeing, when suddenly Sam thought of something that had escaped her notice until now.

The helicopter pilot who'd started the avalanche had seen the horses vanish into the valley. He knew where they were. He could go after them. Not right this minute, maybe, but after the spring thaw he could corner them in the place where they'd always been safe.

Sam stared blindly, not seeing the plastered kitchen wall, but the sides of the tunnel, with its ancient petroglyphs of horses. Horses had been there forever. They couldn't be taken away now.

"Samantha, honey, what are you doing to the tablecloth?" Gram asked, and Sam looked down to see her filthy fingernails clawing the checkered fabric.

"Sorry!" Sam said, smoothing the tablecloth down. "It's just that the helicopter followed the Phantom's herd. They know where he is, and I'm sure Norman White will—"

But when Sam glanced to Brynna for sympathy, she caught her smiling.

"No, he won't," Brynna said. She sounded smug, but that didn't make sense.

Sam shoved her hair away from her eyes. They stung from sweat. Blinking, Sam asked, "What am I missing?"

"Honey, we were saving it for a Christmas morning surprise . . . ," Gram began.

"I can't watch her torture herself," Brynna said.

"The Kenworthys aren't the only ones who've had some good news," Gram said. "River Bend Ranch is about fifty acres bigger than we thought it was."

"What?" Sam asked, bewildered.

"That information has been locked in my"—Gram reached up and knocked her knuckles against her head—"simple brain all these years."

"You know those maps I've been going over for the last few months?" Brynna asked. "Of course you do! Well, I kept running across this little odd crescent-shaped plot that didn't seem to be public or private land, but it turns out that it belongs to us!"

"We have all this land along the La Charla that we've known about and worked, of course," Gram said, "but up in the left corner of our holding, well, my grandfather used to say it looked kinda like a dog wagging its tail. He said he paid a pretty penny for it, too, but it was worth it because of the year-round grazing and water in the secret valley."

Year-round grazing and water in a secret valley. That had to be the Phantom's hiding place, Sam thought. It had to be. And it belonged to them.

That meant . . .

Sam's mind spun with the enormity of what Brynna had discovered. That really, truly meant that the Phantom and his herd belonged to them. As long as the mustangs stayed on River Bend Ranch, they could live free.

Twice Sam tried to talk, but her tongue seemed to stick to the roof of her mouth. Finally, she turned to Brynna in slow motion and asked, "You knew where he was, all this time?"

"I had a pretty good idea," Brynna admitted.

The Phantom didn't have to be tamed to stay safe, Sam thought.

"You're positive it belongs to us?" Sam swiveled in her chair, begging Gram to tell her it was true.

"Absolutely. When we were in town just before

the storm," Gram went on, "one of my errands was to take those maps in and have a little talk with a surveyor." Gram tsked her tongue. "It's been ours for four generations."

"Five," Mrs. Allen said, nodding toward the cradle in the living room.

"Five," Gram repeated with a smile. "Sam, I bet you remember me telling you about the summer cow camp we had up there?"

"I do!" Sam said. "Just a couple of weeks ago when Nicolas was here!"

"I thought it had been lost when I was a child. There was that landslide and it was sealed off."

"I think it has a habit of doing that," Sam said, and something dire in her voice must have set off Brynna's suspicions.

"You do?" Brynna said, frowning. "Why?"

Sam drew a deep breath and shrugged.

"It just kind of looks like that," Sam said.

This was not the time to mention the avalanche. When Dad came in after talking with Jake would be plenty soon enough.

Right now, she wanted to soak up the revelation that the Phantom could stay free.

New Year's Eve festivities were in full swing.

Long tables held more potluck food than they'd all be able to eat, music came from cowboy guitars, and a crackling yellow bonfire burned as tall as the rooftops when Cody Forster, carried by his big sister Samantha, met his neighbors for the first time.

Wearing a white sweater with gold thread knitted into it for sparkle, Sam edged through the crowd, determined to show the baby to Jen first. To do that, she had to walk past Darrell and Ally, because they'd come to the bonfire with the Kenworthys.

Sam was trying to figure out if they were a couple when Ally's voice soared octaves higher than usual. "Oh, he's so cute!"

Jen turned away from Ryan and her dad, then bent to stare at the baby. Cody stared back.

"He's probably only watching the flames reflected in my glasses, but babies this age usually aren't tracking at all. I'd say he's gearing up to be an intelligent little boy," Jen said.

"I know it." Sam accepted the compliment for Cody, then plopped a kiss on his head.

Before she could ask Jen how the plans for Harmony Ranch were coming along, Dr. Scott and Katie Sterling, both wearing sweaters, knit hats, and scarves, crowded close to see Cody.

"You're getting to be an old hand at this birthing stuff," Dr. Scott shouted over a renewed burst of music. "Congratulations."

"Horses are easier," Sam said, then noticed how Katie looked up at Dr. Scott when she laughed.

What was it about New Year's Eve that put romance in the air?

Even Gram and Dallas were standing closer together than usual, she thought, as they talked with Mrs. Allen, Preston, and Mrs. Coley.

"Yes," Mrs. Coley said, "I get to keep my old job. Ryan's asked me to stay on—"

"Lands sake, Helen, what would he have done if you'd said no?" Mrs. Allen whispered.

"And Brynna," Mrs. Coley continued, talking over her friend's gossip, "I hear you've taken a new job!"

"Three of them," Brynna said. "Ranch wife, wild horse advocate, and mama!"

Sam still got chills when she thought of the phone call from Washington, D.C. A prestigious animal rights group had asked Brynna to use her expertise to help defend the rights of wild horses in the legislature. She'd only have to be gone once in a while, but her knowledge would be valuable and appreciated.

When she'd phoned back to accept the job, Brynna had said, "I'll speak for the horses, since they can't do it themselves."

Then she'd made a choking sound, because Sam had bulldogged her with a hug.

"Yep, one thing the women in this family have a knack for," Dad said now, "is stepping up to the plate." The arm he had around Brynna's shoulders gave her a squeeze.

"And hittin' home runs," Darrell said. He punched Sam in the shoulder and Cody, who'd been almost asleep, awoke with a start and began making mewing sounds.

"I'll take him," Brynna said, holding out her arms.

Sam handed the baby over. Darrell looked hurt that he'd wakened the baby and Sam was about to tell him not to worry about it when Darrell's face brightened.

"Hey, Cody, little buddy," Darrell said, turning his face so he could look into the baby's fretful one, "I've got my snowboard with me and that hillside looks like a place for some *extreme* activity!"

"I think he's a little young. Maybe next New Year's Eve," Ally said, shaking her head. "Let's go get some of Luke Ely's chili. I've heard it's the best."

But Sam had decided to have dessert first. With her hands free, Sam headed toward the potluck table to grab a piece of Gram's cherry pie.

She didn't get very far before she heard Preston talking to Dad. "I hear you're in the wild horse sanctuary business now, too," he said, and Sam had to listen to Dad's answer.

She turned in time to see Dad's good-natured grimace.

"They can stay there for now," he said, but Brynna was holding up four fingers and mouthing a word in Sam's direction.

It took Sam a couple minutes to understand she was saying, "Forever."

The music turned wild as Callie, in jeans and a

University of Nevada sweatshirt, joined in on her flute.

Catching Sam's eye, Callie raised her hand from her instrument to give a thumbs-up. Sam clapped in the air, then returned the gesture, because it was the first time she'd seen Callie since hearing her friend had received a college scholarship. Sam had no idea what the zoology professors would think about Callie's chartreuse hair and the rhinestone glittering in her nostril, but she sure wished she could be there to watch.

"Oh, Sam, before you go," Mrs. Allen said, grabbing her sleeve, "I have a note for you from Darby."

"I was kind of hoping she'd change her mind and come," Sam said.

"We were, too," Trudy said, "but that girl has a one-track mind and she's just in love with that sorrel horse."

"We've got the filly up on her feet," Preston said. "And by *we,* I mean Darby, but she stood still long enough for me to get a picture of them together."

Sam stood on her toes, trying to see the photograph, but she missed her chance when Ryan passed it to Jed Kenworthy.

"Don't hog it, Dad," Jen joked when Jed stared at the photo as if spellbound. When she reached for it, Jed held on and tapped it with his index finger.

"I know this horse."

"Dad, she's wild," Jen pointed out.

"Didn't used to be. See that little white splatter marking on her chest? Did you ever see one like it before? Lila!" Jed called for his wife.

"Well, no," Jen said. She looked over at Sam and made a whirling motion next to her head as if her dad had gone crazy.

But Sam wasn't so sure. The golden filly had looked strangely familiar to her, too, although it had been her conformation, not her marking, that she'd noticed.

"Hey, Lila, come take a look at this," Jed yelled again.

Jen's mother was busy showing off a locket her husband had given her for Christmas, but she walked back to him, smiling as she sipped a soft drink.

She took the picture casually, then lowered the soda can from her lips. She jammed the can in Jen's direction, expecting her to take it.

Jen did, and Lila walked toward the fire to inspect the photo in better light.

"It's her! Kitty's foal!" Lila gasped. "The one we sold to Shan Stonerow! Where did she turn up?"

"Wild, according to your daughter," Jed said, jerking a thumb at Jen.

"Don't blame me! She's been running loose on the range for at least a couple years." Jen glanced at Sam for confirmation and Sam nodded, but after that, Sam didn't hear anything else her friend said.

Kitty's foal. Lila's words echoed in Sam's mind.

Princess Kitty's foal had been sired by Dad's mustang Smoke. If Jen's parents were right, that made the golden mustang a full sister to the Phantom. No wonder she'd looked familiar.

All the color and noise of the party spun around Sam as if she were on a merry-go-round.

"Well, isn't that a nice coincidence," Mrs. Allen said, pressing Darby's note into Sam's hand.

But it wasn't nice, Sam thought. Jake's grandfather, Mac Ely, had told her Shan Stonerow's horse-training method consisted of "showing them who's boss." A horse with the same bloodlines as the Phantom wouldn't respond well to such treatment.

". . . tried to break her the hard way . . . ," Jed was saying. ". . . Called her a monster . . . rolling eyes, charging and high-headed . . ."

Sam couldn't catch all that Jed was saying, but none of it was good. The note crumpled in her hand.

"Now, be sure to read that," Mrs. Allen said, seeing what Sam had done. "She's expecting a call from you tomorrow."

"I will. I really like Darby," Sam said. She smoothed the note out. "I was just, uh, thinking of something else."

The front porch light glowed above the empty spot where the Ely brothers and Callie had been playing. They'd deserted their guitars and headed for the food.

Oh no, Sam thought. If she knew those guys,

there'd be nothing left of Gram's cherry pie. She tried to read her note as she headed after them.

"Thanks for the most important day of my life," Darby had written. "My heart belongs to the horses. I won't let you down. Ever. Love, Darby."

Sam's sigh turned into a gasp when a voice next to her said, "Passing the torch?"

"Were you reading over my shoulder?" Sam asked. She gave a regretful glance toward the potluck table before giving Jen a shove.

"Sure I was, and it sounds like you made a big impression on that little girl from Los Angeles."

"It is kind of cool," Sam admitted. Then she thought about what Jen had really said. "But I'm not passing the torch. It's not like I'd let other wild horses who aren't safe like the Phantom just fend for themselves."

"You could move on to bigger and better things," Jen suggested.

"Better than horses?" Sam asked skeptically.

"There's always world peace," Jen said. "A girl's got to have a goal."

"What are you two scheming?" Ryan's smooth voice cut across their laughter. "It's not enough for you that I'm learning to pull myself up by my own boot belt?"

The girls stared at him for a second.

"Straps," Jen corrected him. "I'll have to look up exactly what they are, but the *expression* is 'pulling yourself up by your own bootstraps.'"

"Whatever," Ryan said, and Jen laughed.

"That's one Americanism you got right."

Sam was watching Jen and Ryan wander toward the barn when Jake walked toward her carrying two plates.

"I rescued the last piece for you," Jake said, handing Sam a slice of cherry pie.

"My hero," Sam sighed.

Of course she was joking, but Jake sounded kind of serious when he said, "I been meaning to ask you something."

Serious, but this time nothing was going to stop her from eating her pie.

"What?" Sam asked as soon as she'd swallowed the first bite.

"Did you tell your horse good-bye?" Jake asked.

"Yeah, but he didn't dance in my honor or anything," she said. Then, seeing Jake's shocked expression, she said, "I didn't tell you about the valley!"

And then she did, and Jake rubbed the back of his neck and said, "Guess I got what I deserved, because I didn't tell you about Kit."

"What about him?" Sam asked.

"He's had enough of these parts," Jake said with faked indifference. "He's gonna help his friend Pani run a ranch in Hawaii."

"Hawaii!" Sam shouted, but her disbelief must have surprised him, because even when Kit yelled

Jake's name from the other side of the bonfire, Jake kept staring at her.

"What?" she asked.

Drawing a breath so deep his chest swelled with it, Jake took Sam's hand in his.

She stopped breathing for a second and saw Jake raise his eyebrows as if asking permission.

"Walk over there with me?" he asked.

This time Sam was the one who was speechless, but she squeezed Jake's hand and walked with him.

Surrounded by her friends and family and a future full of horses, Sam was happy. Best of all, her mind held a picture no one, not even Jake, would ever see.

Before she'd left the valley of wild horses, she'd whispered in the Phantom's ear.

The horse had lowered his head to her shoulder and Sam had done what no one had ever done before. She saw the world through a wild stallion's silver mane.

Even as she'd forced her eyes to travel up the soaring rock wall again, she'd told him, "If my way out works, I'll know how to find my way back to you. Zanzibar, this isn't good-bye."

As the stallion's velvet lips had nibbled her hair, Sam knew he understood.

Acknowledgments

Many people contributed their time and expertise to making the world of River Bend Ranch real. I offer my thanks for Dr. Judson Pierce's veterinary advice, Maxine Shane's BLM wisdom, and Chief Brent Harper's fire experience. Annemarie Bajo, R.N., and Kitty Smith, R.N., gave me medical tips; Officer Jim Overton guided me into the world of police horses; Guy Clifton shared rodeo insight above the chutes; and Willa Cline turned wild ideas into websites.

There's no page big enough to list the librarians, teachers, and booksellers I appreciate for shaping a future we don't have to fear.

Amanda Maciel, Elise Howard, Abigail McAden, Cara Gavejian, Colleen O'Connell, Lisa Moraleda, Julia Richardson, and HarperCollins publishing professionals I've never met are so skillful, they make me look good. Artist Greg Call gave each book a beautiful face. My agent Karen Solem encouraged and advised me with patience and brilliance.

I'm grateful to friends who forgive my disappearance into fiction and always welcome me back.

Most of all, every writer should have my family, but—lucky me!—they don't.

An enchanting world . . .
An island full of possibilities . . .
And a very special horse . . .

Phantom Stallion:
Wild Horse Island

From

Phantom Stallion:
Wild Horse Island

#1: THE HORSE CHARMER

In the dream, horses trot alongside her through a jungle. Burnished bay, black, roan, and glimmering gray, they canter under vines that trail over them, leaving their tails strewn with scarlet flowers. Their nostrils flare to smell honey-sweet air. Their hooves thump a wild rhythm while rain patters on overhead leaves that wave like green elephant ears.

Darby follows a red dirt path, though she doesn't know where it leads. Even when the trail slopes down, ever steeper, and the rain's hiss crowds into her ears, she isn't afraid. The horses press all around her.

She is one of them, until the rain stops.

The horses halt.

With undersea slowness, Darby turns to ask them why. Heads tossing, manes slapping their necks, the horses' uneasy milling tells her they can't go on.

She pivots in a shaft of sunlight. Brightness slanting through the treetops spotlights a clearing. It wasn't there a minute ago. Neither was the dollhouse-small shack.

Rain drips from its metal roof. Rust streaks its walls. A white curtain billows out a window and strange music coaxes Darby to walk closer.

The horses watch as Darby's bare feet take her right up to the wooden door.

Slowly, inch by inch, it is creaking open. . . .

"Honey, you really didn't have time for a nap."

Darby Carter's eyes snapped open.

Car keys jingled. Her mom stood next to the couch, smiling down at her. "Your last day at school tired you out."

"I guess," Darby managed, but then her confusion lifted.

Her last day of school—at least for a few weeks—had come in March.

She shook her head, stared at the suitcases and backpack waiting next to the front door, and realized she wasn't in a jungle.

She was in her apartment, but struggling out of the dream was like pushing aside those tropical vines she'd imagined. At last, she sat up and her eyes wandered to the five o'clock news coming on the television.

Panic zinged along her nerves. "We're supposed to leave at five!"

"Yep, let's go," her mom said.

Suitcases stowed, doors slammed, and seat belts cinched, they sped down the block, dared a yellow light to take their freeway entrance, and headed toward the Los Angeles International Airport.

"You can still change your mind," her mom said. Hands gripping the car's steering wheel, she glanced sideways at Darby. "I can turn around," she added, and when Darby didn't respond, her voice turned serious. "Right this minute."

"It's okay, Mom. I want to go," Darby said.

After all, why should she feel homesick? It wasn't like she'd miss the smog, noise, and sirens. Or school.

She and her mom didn't live in the best neighborhood. Darby's middle school was known for rough hallway encounters and a vice principal who thought a rigid dress code could cure just about any problem students had.

Darby had a different strategy. She'd learned that scuttling down the halls with her eyes lowered made her look like a loser and attracted the wrong kind of attention. So, she walked as tall as a five-foot eighth grader could and pretended to search the tide of faces for her best friend, Heather, even when she knew Heather had class on the other side of the campus.

That worked pretty well unless an asthma attack forced her into a bathroom to use her inhaler. There, she faced waves of cigarette smoke—which only made it harder to breathe—or the accusing stares of girls writing lipstick graffiti on the mirrors.

She got the same looks from the kids in class, when teachers required her to answer questions.

She wouldn't, *couldn't*, fake being dumb. Neither could Heather, and that's how they'd ended up friends. Most days they'd split a sandwich between class and the library, then spent their lunchtimes reading. After school they'd e-mail back and forth and talk on the phone about horses.

Darby sighed.

"Do you have all your medicine? What about your ticket?"

"No, Mom, I threw them out the window," Darby joked, but her mother didn't seem to notice. When she leaned forward to squint through the windshield, Darby felt a jab of guilt and checked her backpack pocket for her plane ticket.

Her mother couldn't afford to get the new contact lenses she needed, but she'd spent the money on the flight that would take Darby across the ocean.

Mom, Darby thought, *I'm really going to miss you.* But she didn't say it, and then she couldn't, because brake lights glared in front of them like a thousand red eyes.

Her mother sucked in a breath and made a worried sound before she muttered, "We'll make it," and started scanning the next lane over for an opening.

"You can just drop me off," Darby told her.

She'd turned thirteen. She could make her way through the terminal and figure out where she was going, right?

Darby crossed her fingers, hoping her mom wouldn't take her up on the offer.

"Of course I can't," her mother said, but she didn't sound firm about it. Suddenly she yelled at a driver weaving in front of them, "Hey! Would it kill you to hang up and drive?"

As soon as she'd finished yelling, they laughed. She and Darby both knew that if her mom's cell phone rang and the number displayed was her agent's, nothing, including L.A.'s next big earthquake, would keep her from answering.

Darby's mother was an actress and she'd been waiting for her big break for as long as Darby could remember. That phone tied her to her career and nothing was more important. Darby didn't try to fool herself. She knew part of the reason her mom was letting her ugly duckling daughter go off without her for six months was so she could concentrate on her career.

Mom claimed that when she'd been married to Darby's father, she'd been happy staying with Darby in an apartment above a pizza parlor, but Darby couldn't picture it. And she knew her parents had broken up over Mom's love of acting.

Long black hair swooped around Mom's amber skin, framing exotic eyes. In fact, "exotic and ethnic" was the niche Mom filled for casting directors, though she'd never played a Hawaiian, which was sort of ironic, because that was what she was. At least half.

And that made Darby one-quarter Hawaiian, which no one would have guessed because her stick-straight black hair framed blue eyes. Her heritage would never have been a big deal except that that's where she was headed now. To Hawaii. Not the touristy, white sand beach and big hotel part, either. She was going to the real Hawaii, where her mom had grown up.

Just because Mom swore never to go back there, doesn't mean I won't like it, Darby told herself. So what if her mother—with the exception of a single phone call—had kept her fifteen-year promise never to speak to her father again?

Darby swallowed hard. She was still mad at her mom for hiding half her family from her for her entire life.

Like a freeze frame in a movie, Darby saw herself sitting in the barn on Deerpath Ranch, watching as a beautiful filly kicked and cried, emerging from the sedated sleep that had made it possible for her to be transported from the Nevada range to a barn.

Darby's eyes had followed the gleam of lantern light on the mustang's red-gold coat and tawny mane, as her mom confessed, "Your grandfather isn't dead. You have a great-aunt and a great-grandmother, too, in Hawaii."

And then, it was like fate stepped in.

Her mother's agent called to tell her she'd won a role in a movie shooting on location in Tahiti. If she accepted, she'd be gone for two months, and since Darby couldn't tag along or stay alone in their apartment, her mom gave her a choice.

"You can stay with your dad," she had said. "Or, if you want to meet your grandfather—for you, I'll call him."

Even as she'd watched her mom's mouth form the words, Darby had known this decision would shape her life. She'd stay on a safe, familiar track if she lived with her father and his second family in the same above-the-pizza parlor apartment he'd once shared with her mom.

She didn't think she was gutsy enough to pack her bags and move to Hawaii, to a place where her mom couldn't drive all night to reach her, in an emergency.

But courage came from a weird place. Darby had fallen in love with a mustang. To keep that wild horse, she'd do anything. When her grandfather had invited her to adopt the horse and bring it along to his ranch, Darby knew that doing *anything* meant living with a grandfather she'd never met.

"There's our exit. Hang on," her mom said now, and then they were careening across traffic, missing the other cars by inches.

When her mom drove right past the sign pointing to the parking garage and pulled up next to a curb marked "drop off," Darby felt a tightening in her chest.

"You said it was okay," her mom reminded her.

"It is," Darby insisted. She tried to sound casual.

Her mother must have sensed something was wrong, though, because she ignored the robotic voice telling them this was only a loading zone. She turned off the car and reached across to place her hand on Darby's shoulder.

Darby looked down, frowning as if it took every bit of her concentration to release her seat belt. If her mom got all mushy, they'd both cry.

"You'll love the ranch. You'll be in heaven," her mom insisted, but Darby didn't look up until she added, "And you'll get along with *him* just fine. You're different than I am."

Yeah, Darby thought, *you have enough bravery for two of us. Why didn't you pass any on to me?*

But she didn't say that, only asked, "What does that mean?"

"He loves horses and so do you."

Darby tried to read her mom's mind instead of her happy face. She would have believed her mom if only she hadn't found that crumpled letter in the trash.

"What if loving horses isn't enough?" Darby whispered.

"It will be," her mom assured her. "Horses have given you a new sense of"—she looked up for a minute, as if searching for the perfect word—"determination."

"I don't know."

"What about that horse camp? You bullied me into letting you go off to Nevada—"

"I've never bullied you," Darby began.

"—then you saved that horse—"

"You keep saying that! I didn't save her."

"All I know is, when I got there, I saw this wild mustang gazing at you with love in her eyes. I *did*. And as your grandfather will be more than happy to tell you, you sure didn't get your horse sense from—" Her mom stopped.

They sat quietly, neither wanting to be the first to open the car door and leave the other.

Then a uniformed guard rapped on the car window.

"Okay, sweetie." Her mom leaned forward and kissed Darby's cheek.

As Darby climbed out of the car and closed the door, she noticed the sidewalk was crowded with people going places. The smell of jet fuel mixed with perfume and coffee in to-go cups. Automatic doors into the terminal opened and closed, letting out party-loud noise. And suddenly, excitement replaced her fear.

She could do this.

Darby patted her pockets and checked her backpack. Her book, medicine, ticket, and the little spiral-bound notebook, in which she'd write down Hawaiian words and the names of people, places, and horses, were all where they should be.

She grabbed her suitcases and squared her shoulders just as her mom wrapped her in a hug. Darby clutched the suitcase handles harder. She refused to cry, but she couldn't help one little gulp.

Her mom stepped back, lifted Darby's chin, and flashed her movie star smile.

"I'm not worried about you, baby, and do you know why?"

Suddenly her movie star smile was replaced with a genuine grin. "Because my daughter could never be unhappy in a place called Wild Horse Island!"

Darby lunged forward for a final, breathless hug, and hoped her mother was right.

The flight across the Pacific Ocean went on forever.

It was only after she'd changed planes for the last leg of her journey that Darby unfolded the stiff, moss-green paper she was using as a bookmark and tried once more to smooth out its wrinkles. Yawning, she read the letter one more time.

Dear daughter,

You, Darby, and her horse are welcome here, and I am grateful for the chance to teach her of her family, her aumakua, and horses. You say she is timid, but the picture of her with the pueo-marked horse shows me sleeping bravery. You must remember that it is the grandparents' right to take as hanai the hiapo, but we will let Darby herself decide.

Sincerely,

Jonah

It didn't make any more sense now than it had when she'd found it just a few hours ago. Did her mom speak Hawaiian? Considering how Darby had found the discarded note, she didn't have the nerve to ask. And when she'd tried to look the words up on the Internet, Mom had spotted her, thrown her hands up in frustration, and insisted Darby did not have time to be fooling around on the computer.

The letter held no clues to what the Hawaiian words meant.

Her grandfather's declaration that he saw her "sleeping bravery" was the most confusing part of all. The bravest thing she'd ever done was lie down next to the wild filly in Nevada. But she'd been shaking as she lowered herself into the snow that day.

The sensible part of Darby's brain said she'd just been lucky that the stunned mustang had accepted her. If the filly had tried to bite or strike out with her forelegs, Darby would have scurried out of reach and waited for help.

No, you would not.

Darby settled back in her seat, smiling and her eyes closed. Then she was back in the dream.

She could smell wet earth and warm horses. Flat green leaves were tambourines for a rainstorm and droplets sparkled on black horsetails just out of reach. Huffing grassy breath, the horse on her left snorted a question. A horse on her right rubbed shoulder-to-shoulder with Darby as they trotted together. Hooves thudded and thumped behind her, but her bare toes were safe. Every mare, foal, and stallion made room for her. She was part of the herd.

Until the horses stopped.

Exposed and alone, Darby didn't want to go on without them, but she had no choice. Her feet continued along the trail. They were walking, jogging, taking her to the shabby little house. Even though she didn't know what was on the other side of the door, she was holding her breath as it creaked open and she could see . . .

The jet's wheels slammed down onto the runway and Darby jerked awake.

Twice she'd had that same dream. *Twice.* What did that mean?

Darby tugged at the backpack she'd stuffed under the seat in front of her. She wanted to be the first one off the plane.

She couldn't waste a minute standing around. Not

today, when her horse was waiting for her.

Was the mustang still confused by the truck ride from Nevada to the coast, or terrified by the week spent in a stall on a container ship? About now, the filly should be coming ashore. Would her ears prick up as she tried to make sense of the sounds of metal clanging and the ship's bottom grating on sand? Would she smell strange plants beyond the heavy scents of oil and salt water?

For the wild filly, this was a whole new world. And Darby knew she was the only one who could make it feel like home.